Power Up

ENDORSEMENTS

Reaching kids in the 4-14 window (the ages children are most likely to embrace Christianity) for the gospel is so challenging. As parents, we need open doors to talk about issues of faith with our kids. Jessie has done a wonderful job of skillfully weaving the power of the Holy Spirit into a practical story line that children can relate to. Jessie lives out what she's writing as a mother, mentor and a teacher in her church. As a pastor, I am always looking for tools to help my kids grab ahold of the Bible. *Power Up* is an excellent resource to open conversations with our kids.

—**Mac McElhaney**, Senior Pastor, Rolling Hills Vineyard Church, Valparaiso, Indiana

Power Up is the inspiring story of a young girl's journey of discovering the incredible power of the Holy Spirit while navigating the very real challenges of life. As both a mother and a pastor, I highly recommend this book. *Power Up* is a tool for parents to introduce their children to the beauty and power of the Holy Spirit as well as teaching them the incredible truth of who the Holy Spirit is and how we can partner with Him in everyday life. I have no doubt that Lexi's journey will impact many young readers."

—**Julie Yoder**, Senior Executive Pastor, The Vineyard Church of Central Illinois

One of my deepest desires as a parent is to help my children come into a vibrant relationship with the Holy Spirit from a young age. I believe God longs to partner with our kids and demonstrate their childlike faith. *Power Up* beautifully illustrates the wonderful adventure of getting to know the

Holy Spirit and what can happen in our lives as we learn to obey his prompting. I'm excited to share Lexi's journey with my children!

—Putty Putman, author of *Live Like Jesus* and *Kingdom Impact*, School of Kingdom Ministry Founder

Mattis is able to intertwine a beautiful biblical perspective of the Holy Spirit into a great story for young readers. Readers will be encouraged to grow into a person who loves God and loves others, and live a life that relies on the Holy Spirit.

—Jessica Miller, Children's Minister, Second Church of Christ, Danville, Illinois

"This book was a literal saving grace for our family! My husband and I are currently navigating (sometimes floundering) our way through our oldest daughter's pre-teen stage of life. When you, as an adult, are still working on your relationship with God, it can be difficult to explain to your child how to transfer what they've been taught to their own personal connection to faith. This story really gave us a great start in opening what is now an on-going conversation. Loved it!"

—Jennifer Mitchell, wife, mother of three, behavioral science professional

Power Up

JESSIE MATTIS

ELK LAKE PUBLISHING INC
Plymouth, Massachusetts

Cover and Interior Design: Derinda Babcock

Editor(s): René Holt, Deb Haggerty

Author Represented by Golden Wheat Literary Group

PUBLISHED BY: Elk Lake Publishing, Inc., 35 Dogwood Dr., Plymouth, MA 02360, 2019

Library Cataloging Data

Names: Mattis, Jessie (Jessie Mattis)

Power Up / Jessie Mattis

130 p. 23cm × 15cm (9in × 6 in.)

Description: Lexi is introduced to the power of the Holy Spirit and her life changes. Will the crisis in her family cause her to doubt her new beliefs?

Identifiers: ISBN-13: 978-1-950051-62-5 (trade) | 978-1-950051-63-2 (POD) | 978-1-950051-64-9 (e-book)

Key Words: Children, Church, Family, Relationships, God in Action, Holy Spirit, Siblings

LCCN: 2019940499 Fiction

DEDICATION

To each child who opens this book—you are far more capable than many grown-ups give you credit for. You were my inspiration for writing this book.

Chip, Sophie, Olen, Charlotte, Mom, Dad, Erin, and Josh—this book wouldn't exist without you guys. I love you so much.

God. Jesus. Holy Spirit. It's all for you.

ACKNOWLEDGMENTS

I am incredibly blessed and grateful to have had so many people support me through the making of this book. First and foremost, I want to thank God. Any credit for this story goes straight to him.

Thank you to my amazing husband, Chip Mattis. You held down the fort to give me the time and space I needed to make this book happen, and you never stopped supporting and believing in me. I love you to infinity and beyond. Thanks, babe.

Thank you to my precious kids, Sophie, Olen, and Charlotte. I look at you and I see Jesus-loving world changers. That's the reason I wrote this book—to inspire other kids to be Jesus-loving world changers too. Thanks for putting up with all my time on the laptop. I couldn't have asked for better kids, and I love you more than you could possibly know.

Huge thanks, Dad and Mom (Brian and Sandy Judy), for always helping me believe I can do anything God asks of me. You're simply the best, and I honestly don't know where I'd be without your love, guidance, and prayers. I love you so much.

Thank you to my sister and brother-in-law, Erin and Josh Terry. Erin, this book would never have gotten finished without you spending so much time with my kids and encouraging me to go work on my book. Thanks for that. The kids and I agree—you're the best. (Well, you might have to duke it out with Mom and Dad for that title, ha!) Josh, I appreciate your love and support too. Thanks for loaning me your wife so often. I love you both.

Charity Fulkerson and Jessica Nemecz, where would I be without you two?! I'm so blessed to have forever friends like you. Thanks for your support and encouragement, for speaking truth into my moments of frustration, and for celebrating the exciting moments with me. (Sorry you're second, Jess—I went alphabetically!)

Christal Greene, thanks for your help answering my technical medical questions to make sure the hospital scene was believable.

Big thanks to my agent, Jessica Schmeidler, from Golden Wheat Literary. Thanks for believing in me. Your ongoing guidance, support, and kindness are so appreciated.

The reason this book is not just sitting on my computer, but is now in your hands, is all because a kind publisher named Deb Haggerty took a chance on me and my story. Thank you, Deb, and everyone at Elk Lake Publishing, Inc. for all your hard work on this project. I appreciate you very much.

Getting a book ready for publication is definitely a team effort. Thanks to my editor, René Holt, for working with me and doing all you could to make this book the best it could be.

At my first writing conference (the 2018 Blue Ridge Mountains Christian Writers Conference), I was in tears with discouragement after one meeting. The next day, I met with Nancy Lohr and regained my vision. Thank you, Nancy, for taking me seriously in spite of my inexperience. Your gentle, constructive feedback was exactly what I (and this book) needed.

At the same conference, I met a great man named Tim Shoemaker. After hearing I had been told "nobody's publishing middle grade" by an agent, Tim spoke this truth that spurred me on: "There are thousands of books for broken adults. Why not get them before they're broken?" His passion for reaching children through writing was infectious. Thanks, Tim, I'm forever grateful for your encouragement and teaching.

To the greater Vineyard church (specifically, Urbana and Rolling Hills): Thank you for spreading the naturally supernatural ways of God across the globe, and for empowering children to participate in the Kingdom of God just the same as adults. I wouldn't be who I am today without you, and I never would have been given the vision for this book without the foundation you laid.

To Cornerstone Christian Fellowship: Thanks for taking us in, loving, and supporting us in our shared vision of advancing the Kingdom.

Many other friends and family members encouraged me along the way. Every kind word and inquiry about my writing meant a great deal to me. You know who you are. Thanks for everything.

CHAPTER 1

"Ouch! My hair—get off my hair!" eleven-year-old Lexi shrieked from the back of the car.

"I'm just trying to buckle my booster seat!" Millie, Lexi's little sister, yelled in her own defense. "Sam's books are everywhere, and I don't have enough room!"

"But you're leaning on my hair! Get off!" Lexi squealed in pain, while unsuccessfully trying to free her long, auburn braid from underneath her sister's arm. Lexi didn't usually spend much time on her appearance, but this morning she had spent almost twenty minutes in front of the mirror, trying to braid her hair just right. She had even chosen a blue sweater because her dad once told her the color made her dark-blue eyes sparkle. Now she was getting all rumpled under the weight of her sister's elbow.

Millie stopped what she was doing long enough to set Lexi's hair free, then proceeded to make a face at seven-year-old Sam, as if to blame him and his books for their current predicament. Lexi rolled her eyes as she straightened out her hair and shirt, hoping her mother didn't see. She wasn't in the mood for a lecture.

Lexi Hanson was squished in the back seat of her family's old, black SUV on her way to church. Her parents, Jordan and Linda Hanson, looked forward to going to church each Sunday. Lexi couldn't figure out why. Their drive to church always seemed to consist of running late, bickering, complaining, and more bickering. At least that's how things went in the back of the car.

Sam, Lexi's generally helpful and soft-spoken little brother, liked church too ... but Lexi knew it was mostly because of snack time. Church snacks were a welcome break from the healthy options their mom stocked at home. Millie, who for some reason always had a smile on her face (unless she was screaming mad like a moment before), enjoyed church too. But she usually liked whatever Sam liked. Millie was five and didn't always form her own opinions.

Lexi, on the other hand, was *not* looking forward to church. She already knew practically every Bible story there was to know—she had been hearing them at home and at church since she was born. Besides, Lexi knew exactly how each Sunday morning went.

First, Lexi's family would all pile into the car about five minutes late. Then, her mother would make her weekly speech about the importance of being on time. Although Lexi never intended to participate in the bickering between Sam and Millie, somehow, she always got sucked in, and they would spend nearly twenty minutes arguing in the backseat. When they arrived, they would sign into Kids' Church and proceed to their separate classes, while their parents went with the other grownups to hear the sermon.

Next, Lexi would sit and look at books or talk to the other girls while the rest of the kids in her class played for a bit. When everyone arrived, they would watch a video with some worship songs (always too loud), have a short lesson (which she already knew), and eat a small snack (probably graham crackers again). Then their parents would pick them up, and they'd all head back to the car. Lexi always hoped they could go to Cracker Barrel for lunch. That was the best part of going to church—eating lunch at a restaurant afterward.

As they pulled into the parking lot, Lexi gazed out the window at the sprawling one-story brick church building. Mr. Hanson, always looking for ways to help other people, pulled the car into a parking spot far from the door and shifted the SUV into *Park*.

"We should save the close parking spots for people who need them more than we do," he announced. There was a spring in his step as they hiked across the parking lot. Lexi stuck her hands in her pockets to shield against the chill of the damp, spring morning. When they were about halfway across, a light rain began to fall. Covering their heads with their hands, Lexi and her family jogged inside, her parents exchanging quick hellos with a few adults Lexi recognized.

A friendly voice called out in their direction. "Good morning!"

Lexi looked up from watching her mom use the Kids' Church check-in computer and saw a volunteer named Mandy heading their way.

Mandy trotted up and greeted them each individually. Sam's hazel eyes stared at his scuffed tennis shoes as he mumbled a quiet *hello*. Millie peered through her bouncy, blonde curls, wordlessly smiling at Mandy.

"Good morning," Lexi said in a voice just loud enough to be heard. Being eleven and all, Lexi knew she was expected to return someone's greeting, but she hoped Mandy wouldn't want to keep chatting. She got nervous talking to people she didn't know very well—especially grownups.

Mandy turned to speak to Mr. and Mrs. Hanson as Lexi exhaled her relief.

"Unfortunately, there just haven't been enough volunteers to continue teaching the kids in separate classes," Mandy apologized. "The leaders have decided to combine classes, at least for now, which means the kids will all be together with one new teacher."

Combine the classes? Lexi groaned inwardly. That meant around twenty kids, from age five all the way up to eleven, in one big class. She was used to having a small class with only six or seven kids. If a bunch of younger kids were going to be in class with her, she just knew she was going to be even more bored than usual. Lexi sighed as they walked down the long hall with bright, primary-colored circles painted on the walls and dangling from the ceiling.

Lexi and her siblings were the first to arrive at the classroom. They entered the Noah's Ark-themed room and sat in the circle of empty folding chairs arranged in the center of the large room. Lexi noticed the new seating arrangement right away. Usually the chairs were in rows. She was used to sitting in the second row where she could more easily avoid eye contact with the teacher. Not that she didn't pay attention during class—she just didn't like being called on to answer questions. Now there would be no barrier between her eyes and the teacher's.

As soon as they sat down, a plain but nice-looking young woman, dressed in an oversized burgundy sweater and stylish jeans, walked out from behind a desk to greet them. Black-rimmed glasses framed her soft, green eyes, and she wore the front of her shoulder-length brown hair pulled back loosely in a barrette. She appeared to be around the same age as Lexi's Aunt Hailey, who was in her early thirties. She held an extra-large purple travel mug in one hand as she approached with a smile and a confident stride.

"Good morning! My name is Miss Kate."

CHAPTER 2

Lexi could tell right away this teacher was different from ones she'd had in the past. There was nothing extraordinary about Miss Kate's appearance, but there was something about her Lexi couldn't quite put her finger on. Right away she seemed kind and trustworthy … maybe even a little spunky. But no matter how nice she seemed, Lexi still didn't like the idea of this new big class.

Lexi made herself smile and respond politely to Miss Kate anyway. "Good morning, Miss Kate. It's nice to meet you." She knew her parents would be proud. Lexi had taken most of her life to finally work up the courage to greet adults with more than just a shy smile. It still wasn't easy.

After Sam and Millie returned Miss Kate's greeting, she told them they could play for a few minutes before class began. Sam and Millie jumped from their folding chairs and ran to the toy shelves without delay.

Lexi chose to remain in her seat as Miss Kate strolled back over to the teacher's desk. Lexi glanced around to see Sam talking to some other boys his age. Millie was sitting on the floor next to one of her friends while they played with each other's hair. Lexi was anxious for class to start. The sooner they got started, the sooner they could go out for lunch.

A minute later, Miss Kate seemed to have read Lexi's mind. "Time to get started, class." Miss Kate spoke in a firm but friendly tone as she walked into the center of the circle of chairs. She waited until everyone was seated and mostly quiet before introducing herself to the class.

"Welcome! My name is Miss Kate, and I'm so glad you're here! Due to a shortage of teachers, we'll all be meeting in this room each Sunday—at least for a few weeks." She paced around the room, weaving in and out among the students as she spoke.

"My expectations for this class are simple. Be kind, be curious, and ask lots of questions." She smiled. "We're going to be learning a lot of exciting stuff you won't want to miss!"

Miss Kate walked back to her desk to set down her big, purple mug. Lexi wondered just how heavy it was. "Now let me tell you something about myself, so we can start getting to know each other." Miss Kate's demeanor shifted from business to casual as she returned from her desk and leaned against the tall stool, which stood among the circle of chairs. "Let's see ... I love to laugh, my favorite color is purple, and I run my own bakery here in town." Lexi noticed Miss Kate's inviting smile rarely left her face. "Oh, yes—I am completely in love with Jesus and am so thankful for the Holy Spirit being alive in my life. Okay, now it's your turn!"

They went around the circle introducing themselves, but Lexi hardly heard a word the others said. Instead, Lexi wondered what in the world Miss Kate was talking about. *She's thankful for the Holy Spirit being alive in her life? What does that even mean?*

As far back as she could remember, Lexi had been taught that God was really three beings at the same time—God, Jesus, and the Holy Spirit. It was pretty confusing actually, but she never thought too much about them being three. She believed in God and knew all about Jesus. She had asked Jesus into her heart years ago. If the Holy Spirit was just another part of God, Lexi was pretty sure that was all she needed to know.

When the class finished introducing themselves, Miss Kate began to speak. "Over the next few weeks, we'll be going on an adventure!" She clasped her hands with a pop of excitement. "Not the kind of adventure where we all wear khaki vests and try to outrun wild animals in a Jeep, although that *would* be exciting ..." Her voice trailed off, as if considering the possibility, then she winked. "No, the adventure we're going on is a spiritual one."

Lexi had a feeling she wasn't alone, as she fought the urge to roll her eyes.

Miss Kate looked out across a sea of blank faces and stifled a laugh. "Give it a chance, you guys. We're going to learn some incredible things that may be completely new to you, and it won't matter if you're five or eleven years old—this is good stuff for all ages. You may not believe me yet, but we're going to have fun too!"

Lexi twisted the blue plastic ring she wore on her right index finger. She couldn't decide if she was interested or annoyed. She really didn't think there was much more about God she didn't already know.

On the other hand, there *was* something interesting about this new teacher. It was as if all of Lexi's previous teachers had been bored by the material they had to teach, while Miss Kate seemed to believe it was truly exciting.

Lexi felt herself growing curious about where Miss Kate was going with all this. After all—an adventure? She'd definitely never heard the word *adventure* used to describe church before. She would have to see it to believe it. Right now, the only thing she knew for sure was, whether class was interesting or boring, she would be at Cracker Barrel in an hour and a half (she hoped).

Miss Kate seated herself back on the stool. "Most of you already know that Jesus is the human form of God who lived on earth for a while to show us his love in person. Jesus was arrested and crucified, which means he was hung on a cross to die, even though he didn't deserve it. He died as a sacrifice for us and forgave our sins—the wrong things we do—so those of us who love him could live forever in heaven when our life here is over."

Lexi listened politely but hoped Miss Kate would hurry up and get to something she didn't already know. Her mind was beginning to wander, and her thoughts quickly turned to school. She knew her history grade had been slipping.

Lexi was worried. On Friday, the principal had told her sixth-grade class they would have to earn As and Bs in every subject in order for the school to pay their way for the end-of-the-year class trip. She wasn't sure exactly how low she had let her history grade slip or how much work she'd have to do to get it back up, but she would do whatever was necessary. She would talk to her teacher tomorrow.

If only history wasn't so boring. Lexi shifted in her seat. Why was it she could hear a perfectly good history lesson and three minutes later, forget everything the teacher said? She figured she must have been born without a history section in her brain or something. There had to be some way to stop the material from going in one ear and out the other.

A few chairs down, Sam sneezed, startling Lexi and bringing her thoughts back to class. "Bless you," she whispered to her brother. She decided she'd better start paying attention in case Miss Kate called on her.

"After Jesus was crucified, he was raised from the dead three days later! Isn't that incredible? He stuck around on earth for a few weeks, but then it was time for him to go back to heaven." Miss Kate stood up and her short-heeled boots clicked loudly on the tile floor as she paced around the circle of chairs.

"And now we're getting to the main point of today's lesson. Before he left, Jesus told his followers he would send the Holy Spirit to stay until he returned. We're still waiting on Jesus's return, but just like he said, the Holy Spirit *did* come to earth to be with his followers—including those of us here today who have put our trust in Jesus!"

Miss Kate sure did gesture a lot as she spoke. If Lexi hadn't known better, she would have thought Miss Kate was just learning all this stuff for the first time herself, based on how excited she seemed.

"So that's why and how the Holy Spirit got here in the first place. He has the special job of helping and encouraging us as we wait for Jesus's return. I know he seems a little mysterious since we can't see him, so if it helps, try picturing Jesus, and then think of the Holy Spirit as a wonderful friend like Jesus who we just can't see!"

Well, that's new. The Holy Spirit is sort of like a Jesus that you can't see? Lexi had never heard this explanation before. The idea did sort of help the Holy Spirit seem a little less mysterious, she supposed, even if rather strange.

At least Miss Kate wasn't boring. And even though Lexi had heard of the Holy Spirit, she'd never really considered he might have a special job. Maybe there truly *was* something new to learn from church.

CHAPTER 3

"Let's talk about what all this means for us today," Miss Kate continued. "The Holy Spirit is more than just another name for God. The Holy Spirit is the part of God who lives *in* us when we decide to follow Jesus." Miss Kate's eyes shone with delight.

"But it's not as if he just wants to set up camp in our hearts and stay put the rest of our lives. If we let him, he will start living *through* us." With a genuine smile still stretched across her face, Miss Kate glanced around the room at the faces staring back at her, apparently sensing her enthusiasm wasn't exactly mutual.

"Okay," she said, not at all bothered by the passive faces, "I know this sounds a little weird and maybe doesn't make sense just yet, but stick with me here." She held up her index finger as she paused for a quick sip from her enormous travel mug.

Lexi stared at the mug. *That thing must weigh two solid pounds.*

"Close your eyes for a minute and think about all the power God has," Miss Kate instructed. "Keep thinking … and think about all the power *you* have. Yours can't even compare to the power of God, right?

"Now imagine God decided to give you some of his power. You would probably feel like a superhero!" She struck a Superman pose which made Millie giggle. Lexi, once again, had to fight back an eye roll, while she noticed Sam sit straighter as soon as he heard the word *superhero.*

Miss Kate crouched forward as if about to spill some big secret. "Would you believe me if I told you God gives us the Holy Spirit as a gift, and if we choose to take and use this gift, we will have access to God's power?"

As she stood, her face looked serious, but her eyes crinkled as if she were fighting to hold back her usual smile. "If this all sounds crazy and you don't believe me yet, no worries. God wants you to discover this truth for yourself."

Miss Kate strode to her desk to grab her maroon, leather-bound Bible and quickly flipped to her destination. Lexi wished she knew how to find books of the Bible so easily.

"In the Bible, John 14:12, Jesus says, 'I tell you the truth, anyone who believes in me will do the same works I have done, and even greater works, because I am going to be with the Father.'" Miss Kate looked up and closed her Bible. "After Jesus went to heaven, he sent the Holy Spirit to empower us to do great works, as long as we have faith in him." She leaned in with her hands on her knees. "Pretty incredible, right?"

Lexi glanced around the room. Sam was staring at Miss Kate with wide eyes. She could tell Millie was half listening while gazing at the games on the other side of the room. The other students appeared to be listening to Miss Kate with more interest than they typically showed their teacher.

"The Holy Spirit has different jobs to do," Miss Kate continued, "and one of those jobs is to be a helper. Let's talk a little more about what being a helper means, and then I'm going to give you guys some homework for the week."

Wait, homework? Is she serious? Just when Lexi was starting to think this new teacher might not be so bad, she had to go and ruin things by assigning homework. Lexi had more than enough homework from school and certainly didn't want to spend even *more* of her time studying and writing essays. She, along with the rest of the class, just stared at Miss Kate.

"I hoped you guys would trust me a little more," Miss Kate said with a short, hearty laugh. "I guess I still need to earn your trust. So, in order to put your minds at ease, be assured your homework will *not* be to solve problems on a worksheet. I'll leave those assignments to your school teachers. This homework will be much more interesting."

Lexi could not imagine what Miss Kate possibly had in mind to make homework more interesting.

Miss Kate went on. "The Holy Spirit is our helper. Did you know if you ask for his help, God will help you?" She paused as she looked across the room of faces, some appearing curious, some unsure. "His help may not always be what we expect, but he is a very good God, and he loves to help his children—us!"

Miss Kate settled back onto her tall stool. "So this doesn't get confusing, let me give you some examples of how the Holy Spirit will probably *not* help. Let's say you have a big test coming up, but you don't want to study.

You'd rather play outside all day. Then, you get to school, they pass out the test, and you pray for help to get a perfect score.

"Or, say it's your job to do the dishes after supper, and you pray for God to do the dishes for you. What do you think will happen? Do you think the Holy Spirit will zip down and magically change your test score or clean all the dishes?" Miss Kate's eyes shone as she glanced around, waiting for comments.

The class laughed, and a tall, thin boy named Jacob shouted, "I wish!" which made them giggle even more.

Miss Kate laughed along with them. "Sorry to disappoint you, Jacob, but that's not usually the way God chooses to work.

"So how *does* the Holy Spirit help us? Pretend you wake in the middle of the night, scared from a bad dream. What do you think might happen if you tell God you're scared and ask for his help?" She glanced around the room.

"He'll help us be brave?" one girl ventured, uncertainly.

"He'll take away the scared feelings?" a young boy suggested.

"You guessed right!" said Miss Kate, pleased with the responses. "If you ask him to, the Holy Spirit will comfort you and help fill your mind with good thoughts instead of scary ones."

As she listened, Lexi fiddled with the fringe on the sleeve of her blue sweater. Every once in a while, she had bad dreams and hated waking up her mom and dad. She'd have to remember to try this.

Miss Kate looked around the circle from student to student. "What other things do you think the Holy Spirit could help us with?"

Anna, a girl with long red hair, quickly raised her hand. "Maybe he could give us courage to stick up for a kid who's being picked on at school!"

"Great answer!" said Miss Kate. "What else?"

Jacob spoke up without bothering to raise his hand. "He could sure help me by giving me a thousand dollars!" he said with a smirk. Part of the class giggled while the others looked at Miss Kate, unsure whether they should join in.

Miss Kate smiled but quickly moved past the distraction. "All jokes aside, I think you guys are getting this figured out. Along with comforting us and making us brave, the Holy Spirit can also give us the right words when we aren't sure what to say. He offers his help to us in lots of different ways."

Lexi had never thought about needing supernatural help, but even if the idea was a bit strange, she found herself relieved to know she wasn't expected to do all these things on her own.

Miss Kate went on. "The Holy Spirit loves to help us out. And remember, the Holy Spirit isn't just God's little buddy who goes around doing God's work for him. The Holy Spirit *is* God!"

CHAPTER 4

When the class discussion came to an end, Miss Kate guided the students in a messy craft, involving lots of Popsicle sticks and glue. Part of Lexi thought she was getting a little old for Popsicle stick crafts. The other part of her still loved piling on the glue to build a sticky masterpiece.

After clean-up, Miss Kate led them in praying for each other, which was new. Their previous teachers usually just said a quick prayer at the end of class, but Miss Kate took time to pray for each student, and even invited them to participate. Then came snack time. Graham crackers and water—as usual.

Lexi hoped Miss Kate had forgotten about the homework assignment she'd mentioned earlier. No such luck. Just then, Miss Kate stepped carefully around the craft and snack tables, wiping her hands on the front of the white apron she'd borrowed from the storage closet.

"Okay, boys and girls, it's time for your homework assignment! I know the word *homework* makes you shudder, but please give it a chance. You might even end up *enjoying* it." Miss Kate had a slightly amused look on her face, as if she knew something they didn't.

As Lexi glanced around, the other faces confirmed she was not the only one skeptical about this church homework thing. Aside from the crunching of graham crackers, the room was silent.

"There are two things you should know. First, the homework assignments in this class are for those of you who already follow Jesus. If you don't, I'd love to tell you more about him after class. And second, as your Kids' Church teacher, I honestly can't make you do homework."

Lexi and a few others breathed a sigh of relief. Miss Kate chuckled as she continued, "And while I can't *make* you, I want you to think about doing it anyway. Pray about it, even. Okay, your homework this week is to find a time when you could use a little help, ask the Holy Spirit to help you, and then pay attention to *how* he helps.

"If you try this out and let us know next Sunday how the Holy Spirit helped, you'll get to choose an item from the prize box." Miss Kate gestured like a game show host toward the green plastic treasure chest, sitting in its usual place on the shelf near her desk.

Lexi saw Millie grinning from across the room. She knew Millie loved all the colorful trinkets in the prize box—bracelets, bouncy balls, sunglasses that fell apart before you got home, bookmarks, pencils, and more. Millie's prizes usually ended up broken or lost under her bed, but she loved earning them all the same.

"Everybody understand? Sound simple enough?" Miss Kate glanced around the room to see heads nodding back at her. "All right, you may play until your parents come to pick you up. Have a great week, and I'll look forward to hearing your stories next Sunday!"

Moments later, Mr. and Mrs. Hanson arrived to check their children out of class. As Lexi, Sam, and Millie walked back to the SUV with their parents, Lexi couldn't help but wonder what this week would hold. If the kids in class decided to do the homework, there might be some interesting stories to hear next Sunday. *If* this whole Holy-Spirit-being-alive thing was for real, at least. Lexi wasn't sure if she wanted to do the homework or not. All she wanted to do was get some lunch and rest her brain.

"Who wants to go to Cracker Barrel?" Mr. Hanson asked. Lexi smiled as she high-fived her brother and sister. They piled into the car as fast as they could.

After lunch, Lexi and her family drove home for a restful afternoon of playing basketball in the driveway, making homemade granola bars for the upcoming week's snacks, and reading. Lexi absolutely loved Sunday afternoons. This was the only time during the week when her whole family was home together for more than an hour or two in the evenings.

After beating Sam in a game of H-O-R-S-E, Lexi put the basketball away in the dusty garage, kicked off her blue tennis shoes, and headed upstairs. The only rooms in the upstairs of the house were hers, Sam's, Millie's, and a bathroom. Sometimes, she felt as if they had their own separate house up there.

Lexi entered her room, picked up the only library book she hadn't already consumed, and flopped down on her bed. After rereading the first three sentences several times, Lexi realized she was too distracted to read, so she tossed the book aside and rolled onto her back with her hands folded behind her head, thinking. Thinking about school.

Lexi was a good student, typically earning all As and Bs on her report cards, but this semester was different. She hadn't told her parents yet because she wasn't sure, but she was afraid she might be failing history.

She really did try in class (although she could always try a little harder). She just couldn't find a reason to *care* about all those dates and people and wars that happened so long ago. *Really, why does it matter so much? It's over, in the past—history, after all.*

Somehow, she would have to force herself to care. And anyway, why would the school only pay for the kids who got As and Bs to go on the trip? It didn't seem fair. But if she had anything less on her report card, she knew she'd be staying home. Her parents would let her go if the trip were paid for, but they didn't have money in the budget to cover the cost themselves.

Lexi could hardly contain her excitement just thinking about the trip. Three days at Six Flags in St. Louis, Missouri, with her friends—and lots of chaperones, of course. They'd get to stay in a hotel, go swimming, and eat corn dogs and cotton candy all day. They'd play games and ride roller coasters until they were sick, stay up late talking and laughing until they finally fell asleep in the fluffy hotel beds, and then get to wake up and do it all over again! Missing the fun was definitely not an option.

She sighed dreamily, imagining the excitement—being away from home with her friends for three whole days. Lexi knew the first thing she had to do was find out what she needed to do in order to earn at least a B in history. She'd ask her teacher the next day. There would probably be extra credit assignments involved. She would force herself to care about history if it took every last ounce of her brain strength.

CHAPTER 5

Lexi rolled off her bed and bounded down the stairs, taking them two at a time. Suppertime was approaching, and she saw her mom had just set popcorn, fresh vegetables, and grapes in the middle of the kitchen counter. Lexi's mother cooked a lot during the week, and on Sunday evenings she declared supper a free-for-all, meaning they were allowed to eat anything they wanted—almost. Lexi, Sam, and Millie thought it was awesome.

Sam and Millie joined Lexi in the kitchen and began sorting through the fridge, filling their plates with all sorts of interesting choices. Mrs. Hanson stood back and watched with a half-smile. Lexi grinned at her mom as she walked into the living room, her plate full of popcorn, two baby carrots (to prevent a scolding about the importance of eating vegetables), a cheese stick, three pieces of leftover bacon, and a big spoonful of strawberry jam.

Usually on Sunday evenings, they ate their meal while watching a nature show as a family. Tonight, though, as they all got settled in the living room, Lexi's parents brought up the topic of church. Lexi hadn't thought much about church all afternoon, but suddenly the new ideas Miss Kate had talked about came flooding back to mind. She listened as Sam told their parents about the morning.

"We have this new teacher, and her name is Miss Kate. She seems nice so far. She helped us do a fun craft with Popsicle sticks, but we couldn't bring them home today because the glue had to dry."

"That sounds fun, Sam!" Turning to her younger daughter, Mrs. Hanson asked, "Millie, how did you like church today?"

"It was great! They put all our classes together into one huge class, so I got to be with the big kids!" Millie beamed with pride as Mrs. Hanson leaned over and kissed the top of her head.

"And how was class for you today, Lexi?"

Lexi thought for a moment. She really wanted to just turn on the TV and get the show started, but she decided to answer honestly. "Pretty good, I guess. Miss Kate seems nice. She's really smiley. She talked a lot about the Holy Spirit and how he can be our helper when we're sad or scared. Stuff like that." She paused. "Do you guys think the Holy Spirit really does those things?"

Lexi's parents looked thoughtful. After a few seconds, her father answered simply, "I suppose he does. Anyway, I'm glad you like your new teacher."

Well, that's not much of an answer. Maybe there's more to know about the Bible and the Holy Spirit than even Mom and Dad know. How strange to think Miss Kate might be teaching things even her parents were unsure about.

Lexi decided not to mention the church homework assignment to her parents. Sam and Millie seemed to have forgotten because they didn't bring up the subject either. Maybe she would experiment with the homework assignment. Lexi felt a new curiosity to find out for herself whether or not this Holy Spirit stuff was real.

Mr. Hanson flipped on the nature show, and they ate their mismatched meals in silence. Lexi learned more than she ever cared to know about the migration patterns of Canadian geese.

CHAPTER 6

Monday morning, after a noisy, twenty-minute ride, the school bus pulled up in front of the old brick school building. Lexi hopped down the three narrow steps to the pavement with a quick wave to the bus driver. She hoped she had time to get inside and talk to her friends for a few minutes before the bell rang.

Lexi was one of only twenty-four sixth-grade students at Washington Grade School. She and her family lived in a southern Indiana town too small to have a separate middle school, which meant kindergarten through eighth grade met in the same building. Mr. and Mrs. Hanson were pleased to have all three of their children under the same roof during the school day, but Lexi still wished there was a separate middle school.

Weaving skillfully through the crowd of students, Lexi arrived at her locker where she found Claire and Eliza waiting.

"Hey, guys! How's it going?"

Claire shifted her backpack from one shoulder to the other. "Not bad. How was your weekend?"

Lexi remembered the looming class trip. "Fine, except I just realized yesterday I'm going to have to get my history grade up fast if I want to go to Six Flags with you guys." Claire was a straight A student, and Eliza got Bs and Cs. Claire's way was sure to be paid by the school, and Eliza's parents had already told her they'd pay. Lexi was the only one whose fate was up in the air.

"I need to talk to Mr. Drye and find out exactly what I'll have to do to earn at least a B by the end of the semester," she said.

Mr. Drye. What a perfect name for a history teacher. A Drye name for a dry subject. Lexi sighed.

Eliza tried to encourage her. "Don't worry, Lexi. I'm sure you'll get to go. You'd better—the trip wouldn't be the same without you! The rides, the hotel, the freedom from chores and parents for three days ..." They laughed as they high-fived each other, and Lexi's spirits began to rise.

"Thanks," said Lexi. "I'll do everything in my power to get my grade up. I only wish I hadn't wasted half the semester." She regretted all the times she chose to read a book or play basketball instead of studying her history homework. "Okay guys, I have to go catch Mr. Drye before the bell rings. See you later!"

Lexi darted around students in the busy hallway and quickly found the history classroom. She poked her head inside the open door as she knocked. The classroom was empty, except for Mr. Drye, who was sitting behind his large, brown desk.

He looked up from the stack of papers piled high in front of him. "Come in!"

"Good morning, Mr. Drye," she said politely. She took a seat in the yellow plastic chair opposite his desk, which was covered with papers, red pens, and an assortment of random supplies. Lexi couldn't see any rhyme or reason for the way the desk was organized, but Mr. Drye had let the class know everything was in just the right spot.

"Good morning, Lexi. What can I do for you?"

"Well ..." She hesitated, not knowing exactly what to say. "I need to get my history grade up to a B. I'm not sure what my grade is right now, but I was wondering if you could tell me what I need to do over the next few weeks to earn a B ... please."

Mr. Drye looked at her. "Lexi, your grade has been steadily slipping over the past month or two. You're usually a focused student, but you just don't seem to be applying yourself to your full ability." Compassion took over his gaze as he tapped his pen on his desk. "Hold tight just a moment while I think."

Lexi sat quietly, barely breathing as Mr. Drye pulled some papers from a drawer and checked the numbers in his grade book. Her pounding heart echoed in her ears. Had her grade really dropped so much? Was he going to say there was no hope? Tears threatened as she waited for what seemed like forever while Mr. Drye concentrated on whatever he was looking at.

Finally, he looked up and spoke. "Your current grade is a C-. In order to have a B soon enough to apply to your class trip—which I'm assuming this is all about—you'll need to receive an A on every new assignment for the next two weeks, as well as on an extra credit assignment." He laid down his pen.

Lexi let out the breath she didn't realize she was holding. She was glad she wasn't failing, at least, but she honestly hadn't realized how far behind she had let herself get. Mr. Drye's words, "you don't seem to be applying yourself," were etched in her mind. And an A on every new assignment? Was it even possible?

Yes. It had to be. Getting less than a B wasn't an option.

Lexi's week was filled with worksheets, art projects, extra history homework, and music lessons. (She was excited to finally learn to play flute.) The church homework assignment completely slipped her mind until Wednesday morning recess, when Miss Kate's instructions popped into her head.

That day, Lexi and her friends were practicing cartwheels as usual. Lexi had grown up with her classmates, Eliza and Claire, and whenever they had outdoor recess, they met up in the grass near the monkey bars. Soon, Eliza and Claire began talking about Abbi, a girl in their class. Abbi's name often came up in their playground conversations.

Lexi knew better than to make fun of people, even behind their backs, but she never exactly *meant* to make fun of Abbi ... there was just so much about her that was different. Pointing out those differences—and sometimes laughing—was so easy when she was around her friends.

"Did you guys see Abbi's project in art class yesterday?" Eliza was laughing. "She used so much glue it will probably take a year to dry. A two-year-old could have done a better job!"

"Yeah," Claire said, "She's never been good at art. The drawing of a dog she tried to do last week was hilarious—did you see? It looked more like a meatloaf with legs!"

Claire and Eliza laughed as they remembered Abbi's feeble attempts at art. Lexi felt a little guilty, but was used to laughing along with her friends when the subject of Abbi came up. She convinced herself pretty easily there was no real harm in laughing.

For some reason, this time was different. Instantly, Miss Kate's lesson about the Holy Spirit slammed into Lexi's thoughts, and she felt a strong need to speak up.

"Uh ..." Lexi stammered, "... maybe we should ease up on Abbi a little bit. I'm starting to feel bad about laughing at her so much. I know I wouldn't like people laughing at me behind my back."

Eliza and Claire paused, which made Lexi a little sick to her stomach. She wasn't sure how her friends would respond. They might be mad. What if they didn't want to hang out with her during recess anymore? What was she supposed to do then? She supposed she would have to start bringing a book and reading alone on one of those concrete benches by the school building. Maybe then no one would notice she didn't have any friends.

Eliza's voice burst into her thoughts. "Are you serious, Lexi?" She was scowling. "Since when do you think you're so much better than us?"

"No—that's not what I'm saying at all!" Lexi could feel her face begin to flush. "I just realized, all of a sudden, how Abbi would probably feel if she ever overheard us, and I thought we might want to stop talking about her. I never said I was better than you!"

The conversation wasn't going at all how Lexi had hoped. She was sure there was no way Eliza and Claire would want to hang out with her now. Recess was beginning to look very bleak for the rest of the year.

To Lexi's relief, Claire came to her defense. "You know, she may be right. I heard Abbi's parents got divorced over the summer, and she's always having to babysit her little brother after school. I guess she does have kind of a hard life. She's definitely a little strange sometimes, but maybe we should lay off."

Lexi shot Claire a grateful look, thanking her with her eyes.

Eliza rolled her eyes and sighed. "Fine." She reached both hands behind her head to fix her long, brown ponytail which had come loose from all the cartwheels. "I guess I'll try to lay off Abbi."

Lexi overflowed with relief. "Thanks, guys. I'm so glad you understand. I just started feeling so *guilty* ..."

Wait. Was this what Miss Kate was talking about? Could the Holy Spirit have been making her feel guilty so she would speak up and do the right thing? And was the Holy Spirit possibly the reason her friends weren't mad at her?

Suddenly, Lexi was looking forward to telling Miss Kate about this experience at church on Sunday. She wanted to see what Miss Kate thought. Lexi needed to find out if she had really, truly experienced the Holy Spirit working through her or if it was all just in her mind. She was confident Miss Kate would know the difference.

CHAPTER 7

The rest of the week was a typical blur of school, chores, and flute practice. The only difference was the extra effort Lexi had applied to studying history. First, she tried to convince herself that learning history was important, but when that strategy failed, she took to rereading certain passages in her book over and over until she had them almost memorized.

Saturday finally arrived, and Lexi was able to push those things to the back of her mind. Gazing out the window at the afternoon shadows, Lexi settled onto her unmade bed and let her mind drift.

She tried not to think much about the incident from recess a few days ago, but couldn't stop herself. Eliza and Claire had been her buddies since kindergarten, and she didn't want to imagine life at school without them close by. She was grateful her friends weren't mad, and life could go on as normal.

As Lexi's thoughts continued to wander, she realized even though they had grown up together and she considered Claire and Eliza good friends, she didn't really know them very well. Sure, she knew their favorite colors, foods, and subjects, but as she sat on her blue comforter, lost in thought, she began to wonder more about them.

Did her friends dream about what they wanted to be when they grew up? Did they ever travel or go camping with their families? Did they go to church or even believe in God?

Lexi hugged her favorite purple pillow over crossed legs. How strange she had never stopped to ask these questions before. She felt a pull from deep inside to start getting to know Claire and Eliza better. *Three days together in St. Louis should do the trick.* She pressed her face into the pillow and grinned, thinking of all the fun they'd have together. Her smile quickly faded. She really needed to get started on her extra credit report.

Lexi's thoughts were interrupted by a knock on the door. In walked Millie without even waiting for Lexi to shout "come in," like usual.

"What do you want?" Lexi's annoyance showed through squinted eyes.

"I just wanted to see what you were doing, that's all." Millie, with her typical smile, glanced around the room in a way Lexi could only describe as suspicious. "See ya!" Millie shouted as she dashed off.

Well that was weird. Lexi sighed. As far as little sisters went, Millie was a pretty good one, but sometimes she could be completely exasperating.

Lexi turned back toward her window, which was framed with ruffled, pale blue curtains, speckled with small, white flowers. Maybe she would ask to pick out new curtains for her birthday. She was starting to feel a bit too old for all the ruffles.

Her eyes were drawn to a fly, trapped between panes of glass. She felt sorry for him. And then she felt a little sorry for herself. Why did her mind automatically start to wander when she tried to think about history? These next few weeks were going to be tough, for sure.

"Lexi!" her mother called up the stairs, jolting Lexi back to reality. "Time for supper!"

Forgetting about the fly and history, Lexi dashed down the stairs to the table. The dining room was really just an extension of the kitchen, but her parents referred to the space as the dining room anyway. Lexi's growling stomach reminded her she had forgotten her usual afternoon snack.

As the family took their seats around the table, Mrs. Hanson served up helpings of salmon, sweet potatoes, and broccoli. Lexi was thankful she was finally starting not to hate salmon.

"God, thank you for this day, for granting us good health, and providing this food. Bless the rest of our evening together. We love you and praise your name. Amen." Mr. Hanson looked across the table at his family as he picked up his fork. "How was everyone's afternoon? Did you kids get your homework done?" He stabbed his fork into a large bite of broccoli, dripping with butter.

"Yep," answered Sam.

"Yeah," replied Millie.

"Uh-huh," Lexi said.

"And everybody got their Saturday chores done, right?" Mrs. Hanson asked, as she passed out the nearly-forgotten napkins.

"Yes," Sam answered.

"Yeah," Millie said.

"Uh … oops." Lexi had totally forgotten to pick up and dust the living room like she was supposed to do every Saturday. Now she knew she was in for an extra chore as her punishment. And a talking-to. Oh, how she disliked getting a talking-to.

"What do you mean, Lexi—did you forget?" Sam piped up. "The living room was all clean when I was in there a little bit ago."

Lexi glanced quickly around the table in confusion and detected a gleam in her sister's clear blue eyes. Millie made eye contact with Lexi and gave her best attempt at a wink.

"Oh … yeah. I meant 'oops' because I … I wasn't sure if the dusting mitt got put away … my chores are all done," Lexi stammered. Her parents looked confused and rightly so. Lexi felt just as confused as they looked. She hoped this didn't count as a lie. She didn't *think* she was lying. Not technically, anyway.

"Well, as long as the chores are done, I'm happy. Now everybody eat up, and we'll have time to play a round of Clue before bedtime!" Lexi's mom smiled, but the look on her face clearly meant "I know something weird is going on here, but if the chores are done and nobody's arguing, I'm going to let it be."

Lexi finished her broccoli, clearing her plate in record time. After helping clean up the kitchen, she ran upstairs to find Millie playing with Sam in his room. They were on the floor, putting together his new, three hundred-fifty-two-piece superhero Lego set. Lexi hesitated in the doorway. Every time she took a step in Sam's room, she inevitably poked her foot on a tiny, stray Lego. She usually avoided going into his room for that very reason.

"Millie, you cleaned up the living room for me?" Lexi asked. "How come?"

Millie turned toward Lexi, who was leaning across the doorway, still being careful not to step inside. "Because tomorrow we have church again, and I wanted to be a helper like the Holy Spirit, just like Miss Kate told us. I knew you forgot about your chores, so I thought I'd help you, and then you wouldn't get in trouble. Now I'm done with my church homework, and I'll get a prize from the prize box!" Millie looked proud of herself.

That explained it. Lexi wasn't exactly sure this was what Miss Kate meant when she assigned the homework last Sunday, but why argue? After all, her chores were done by someone other than her, and she didn't have to sit through another talking-to.

"Thanks, Sis. That was really sweet of you." Lexi took a cautious step inside to give Millie a quick hug. "Now come on, let's go play Clue! Race you downstairs!" They took off for the living room with Sam dashing to the front as usual. Lexi slowed just enough to let Millie slide around and pass her.

"I beat you, I beat you!" Millie shouted back in triumph. Lexi just grinned as she took her place around the coffee table and began setting up the game, mentally promising herself she'd work on her history report once the game was finished.

CHAPTER 8

Lexi woke up on Sunday morning to the smell of her dad's famous—at least in their house—biscuits and gravy, wafting up the stairs. She figured any day beginning with biscuits and gravy would have to be a good day. Then she remembered history. She had fallen asleep working on her report last night, and the topic was still fresh in her brain.

Lexi had chosen to do her extra credit report on the Revolutionary War, and after making a trip to the school library on Friday, she was well stocked with books to use as sources. Before bed last night she had skimmed through several of them, looking for important information. She had made some progress and was feeling good about the report so far, but she would have to think about it more later. This morning was church, and more importantly, biscuits and gravy were waiting.

Lexi stared into her closet for nearly five minutes, trying to decide what to wear. She finally settled on black leggings with a long green shirt and gray boots. She fastened her cross necklace that Grandma and Grandpa had given her for Christmas around her neck and followed the aroma of biscuits and gravy downstairs.

After finishing a delicious breakfast and spending at least fifteen minutes searching for the hairbrush, all five members of the Hanson family were ready for church. They were about to walk out the door when Millie couldn't find her left shoe. Mrs. Hanson sighed deeply, even though they were only running a tiny bit late this time. The entire family searched for the absent pink sandal until Sam made the discovery in the living room behind the large potted plant where Millie had attempted to hide to avoid getting her hair brushed. Finally, they loaded up and were off to church.

Although the morning had gone pretty much the same as always, this Sunday felt different. Maybe because, for once, Lexi was actually glad to go to class. She was looking forward to the other kids sharing their homework stories. She hoped she wasn't the only one who did the homework. She chuckled at the memory of Millie sneakily doing her chores for her. *At least Millie will have a story to share too.*

When Lexi, Sam, and Millie arrived at their classroom, they found a few other kids already playing. Miss Kate was glancing over some papers at her desk, but when they entered the room she smiled warmly and strolled over to greet them.

"Let's see if I remember …" She slid her glasses to the top of her head and tapped her fingers on her chin. "Lexi … Sam … and Millie. Am I right? Sometimes I'm not great at remembering names." Miss Kate shot them an apologetic look with a half-smile.

"Good job! You're right!" Millie confirmed, flashing her own big smile.

"Excellent, I'm learning! You three may go ahead and play for a few minutes before class gets started." Millie and Sam ran straight to the coloring table while Lexi stayed seated, preferring to be alone for a few minutes before the classroom got loud and busy.

Lexi was nervous to share about how she stuck up for Abbi at school. She didn't know what to expect, and she was afraid of being laughed at. Maybe her story wasn't good enough to share, or maybe she misunderstood what Miss Kate asked of them and had done the homework completely wrong.

Lexi realized she needed to stop worrying, or she would be too nervous to share her story at all. She distracted herself by attempting to silently recite the alphabet backward. Her dad could perform this trick quickly, and his skill never failed to impress her. She recited only from *Z* to the letter *V* before giving up in frustration. *How does he make it seem so easy?*

Finally, Miss Kate called the class to their seats. "Last week we began learning about the Holy Spirit. We learned the Holy Spirit is God and he is also a helper. Who can remember something else we talked about?"

Anna flipped her long, red hair over her shoulder as she raised her hand. "We learned different ways the Holy Spirit can help, like making us brave, helping us know what to say, and helping us feel better when we're scared." She smiled with satisfaction. Lexi could tell she was one of those girls who always liked to be first with the right answer.

"Thank you, Anna. What a great review!" Miss Kate replied. "And now let's move on to the homework from last week!"

Lexi felt a flutter in her stomach. She didn't like speaking in front of others.

Miss Kate continued. "Last Sunday I asked you to find a time during the week to let the Holy Spirit be your helper. Who tried and wants to share their story with the class?"

Lexi looked around. She wanted to share, but she *really* didn't want to go first. Thankfully, Millie's hand shot straight up.

Lexi listened as her little sister told the story of secretly helping Lexi do her chores so Lexi wouldn't get in trouble for forgetting. She wondered what Miss Kate would say. She was pretty sure Millie's story wasn't quite what Miss Kate had in mind when she gave the assignment.

Miss Kate's response surprised her. "Excellent, Millie! Sometimes the Holy Spirit gives us ideas of how another person needs help, and you did a good job of listening."

Millie smiled proudly as Miss Kate turned back to the rest of the class.

"Who wants to go next?" she asked, making eye contact with several different students, her eyebrows raised.

Lexi listened to a couple of other kids share their stories. Suddenly, Sam spoke up. Lexi turned her head toward her brother in surprise. She didn't even realize he had remembered to do the homework.

"One night, I woke up from a bad dream and kept having scary thoughts," Sam said quietly, staring down at his red shoes. "I almost went downstairs to get my mom, but then I remembered what you said about the Holy Spirit wanting to help us feel better when we're scared. So I told him I felt scared and needed help. I wasn't sure if he could hear me." He paused.

"But all of a sudden, I thought about playing at my grandparents' house. I love going to their house. And then I remembered a funny joke my dad told me. I didn't feel scared anymore, as long as I kept remembering good things. And good things kept popping into my head! I fell back asleep and never even had to get my mom. Do you think the Holy Spirit helped me?" Sam asked, looking up from his shoes to meet Miss Kate's kind gaze.

"I absolutely think so, Sam. Well done! You remembered to ask the Holy Spirit for help even in the middle of the night." Miss Kate gave his shoulder a gentle squeeze as she walked behind him.

Just then Jacob spoke up. "These stories sound great and all, but this stuff just doesn't work for me. I mean, I believe in God, but what about when the Holy Spirit *doesn't* help? I was walking home from school last week when this big kid started following me, yelling mean things. I asked the Holy Spirit for help, just in case, but he didn't. The kid followed me all the way home, calling me names until I got inside and locked the door. I guess I'm not good enough for the Holy Spirit to help me," Jacob finished flatly. He looked up at Miss Kate through his shaggy, brown hair, his eyes showing a hint of defiance. Obviously, he was not expecting her to understand.

"Oh Jacob, I'm so sorry," said Miss Kate. "This may surprise you, but I can honestly say I know how you feel." Lexi glanced around the room and saw looks of surprise similar to her own.

"I haven't been in your exact situation before, but there have been times when I've asked for God's help, and it hasn't come the way I asked." Miss Kate's boots clicked in time with her steps. Abruptly, the clicking came to a stop. Lexi could tell Miss Kate had grown serious as she looked across the room.

"There was a time I even got mad at God and convinced myself a good God wouldn't let bad things happen. Sometimes I still get confused. But let me tell you what I've learned over the years, and maybe someday this will help you too." Miss Kate pulled her tall stool into the circle of chairs and perched on the edge.

Lexi glanced around and noticed even Millie had stopped swinging her feet and was sitting up taller, paying close attention.

"The first thing to remember is that God is always good. Always. Even when bad things happen, the fact that God is good never changes. He always knows best, even when we think we know better.

"Unfortunately, we live in a world where bad things sometimes *do* happen, but it doesn't mean the bad things are God's fault. And when they do happen, Romans 8:28 promises us God works out *all* things, even bad things, for good—which is pretty awesome to think about!" Her face brightened, mirroring the hope the verse conveyed.

"The second thing is that God is always with us. This means when bad things happen, God is right by our side the whole time. He carries us through the hard times and gives us supernatural strength and peace. Isn't this incredible?" Miss Kate's passion was undeniable.

"Sometimes during hard times, we feel fear or doubt creeping into our minds. We may have to pray again and again, but God's peace always wins when we keep asking. You'll understand more and more how important this is as you get older."

Lexi had a feeling Miss Kate must have gone through some tough times in order to speak this passionately about God.

"And lastly, I've learned no matter how hard I try, I will never be able to understand exactly how God works." Miss Kate paused for a quick sip of coffee.

Lexi was surprised by Miss Kate's words. *Is she really saying she doesn't understand how God works? Aren't grown up Christians supposed to know all that stuff? It sure would be a relief not to have to understand every single thing about how God works.*

Miss Kate set her purple mug on the empty chair beside her and continued. "This means I must take what I believe to be true about God—he is always good—and have faith, or trust, that his goodness is true even when I don't understand. Admitting I can't always understand God has been very comforting to me in difficult times, especially when I remember he is always good. Then I don't feel like I constantly have to figure him out."

Lexi took a deep breath and shifted in her chair. Miss Kate's excitement made Lexi want to keep listening, but her mind was full, and they hadn't even gotten to the new lesson yet. Lexi could see the other children becoming fidgety as well.

"Now listen carefully a little longer, and we'll have a snack soon," Miss Kate promised as she held out a finger, calling them back to attention. She cleared her throat. "There is an Enemy in the world who *does* want bad things to happen—you've probably heard him called Satan or the Devil. The Enemy wants to keep us from trusting God, so we'll be too miserable and confused to tell others about God's love.

"Even though God has *more* power, the Enemy does have *some* power for now, which is how he makes bad things happen sometimes. You see, there is a war going on between God and the Enemy. God wants us to love and follow him, and the Enemy tries his best to keep that from happening. But this war is not a war we can see—it's a spiritual war."

Miss Kate stood and made her way over to where Millie and a few other five-year-old children sat. "Please, please don't let all this scare you."

She spoke to the entire class but directed her words especially to the littler ones. "Because here's the best part—in the end, God wins the war, and the Enemy will go away for all time! In the meantime, we have his Holy Spirit to help us." A victorious smile covered her face. Lexi glanced around the room and found all eyes glued to Miss Kate again. Her confidence and joy were contagious.

Miss Kate sobered as her eyes focused back on Jacob. "I'm so sorry the Holy Spirit didn't show up the way you asked him to, Jacob. But I can assure you, he was with you the whole time, and I really, *really* hope you'll give him another chance."

Miss Kate stopped and looked around as if she had startled herself by sharing so much. Jacob looked surprised as well, but his expression showed he genuinely appreciated Miss Kate's understanding.

"I know this is a lot to think about, and I realize some of you are still very young, which makes everything even harder to understand. Just know this is true: God loves you no matter what, and God is good no matter what. This is important to remember, and since they say you're more likely to remember something if you repeat it three times ..." She lifted her arms dramatically, then instructed, "Everybody stand up and repeat after me three times! Ready?"

The class jumped up and loudly repeated after Miss Kate: "*God loves me no matter what, and God is good no matter what!*" Lexi and the older students couldn't help but giggle as the younger kids danced around, doing their best to repeat the words in spite of forgetting many of them. After the third repetition, everyone collapsed back into their chairs in fits of laughter.

CHAPTER 9

After giving the students a minute to jump around and "get the wiggles out," Miss Kate called the class back to order. "Who else has a homework story to share?"

Lexi was the only one left. She hesitantly raised her hand.

Miss Kate gave her a short nod, and Lexi took a deep breath to steady her nerves. "I was hanging out with my friends at school like always, and they started making fun of this other girl in our class behind her back. I guess I've made fun of her before too—a little—but this time it felt really wrong.

"I started feeling guilty, and then remembered what you said last week about the Holy Spirit helping us do the right thing. So I told my friends I thought we should stop making fun of her. I was afraid they'd be mad, but they actually ended up agreeing with me! I was so relieved."

Lexi thought Miss Kate might be disappointed in her, after she admitted she'd made fun of this girl in the past, but instead Miss Kate beamed. "You showed great courage in sticking up for your classmate, Lexi."

Lexi's pounding heart began to slow as relief took over. She relaxed into her chair with a satisfied smile on her lips while Miss Kate got out the green treasure chest and passed the prizes around as promised. Lexi saw Millie wiggling excitedly in her chair. She knew this was the moment her sister had been waiting for all week.

Lexi watched Millie dig excitedly through the prize box and finally select a small rainbow notepad. When Lexi's turn came, she examined the contents of the box and settled on a pink pen covered with tiny pictures of kittens.

Miss Kate took a seat. "Let's move to today's lesson. I realize the homework portion went a little long, so we'll keep the rest fairly brief. Today we'll learn about how the Holy Spirit is an encourager."

An image of a cheerleader holding pom poms flashed through Lexi's mind. A cheer she learned from their grade school basketball games popped into her head. *Go, go, G-O, go team go!* Surely that wasn't what Miss Kate meant, although imagining the Holy Spirit as a cheerleader was pretty funny.

"Besides being a great helper, did you know the Holy Spirit is also a great encourager? In fact, he's the most encouraging encourager you could ever imagine!" Miss Kate exclaimed with a grin. The class giggled, although they knew she wasn't joking.

"One way he encourages is by reminding us of the truth when we tell ourselves lies."

Surprise plastered the students' faces, and she continued, "Maybe you didn't realize this was the case, but we all tell ourselves lies once in a while—things that are simply untrue. Just think to yourselves if any of these examples sound familiar:

'I'm not smart enough for this math lesson—I'll never understand.'

'I'm sure my parents wish I could be more like my brother or sister—they're so perfect.'

'God probably couldn't love somebody like me.'"

Miss Kate looked around the room as faces slowly turned from confusion to understanding. "Am I the only one who has thoughts like these from time to time?" she asked with a shrug.

Heads cautiously shook all around the room.

"Thinking like this occasionally is common, but do you know what? They're all lies! The Enemy *wants* us to believe wrong things like this because his job is to discourage us. Thank goodness we have the Holy Spirit to speak truth to our hearts and minds. We wouldn't want the Enemy to win, would we?"

Jacob spoke up, again not bothering to raise his hand. "So you're saying if we think those sorts of things a lot, we're helping out the Enemy?"

"You're exactly right, Jacob. And this is why we need the Holy Spirit's encouragement every day."

Lexi tried to read the faint expression on Jacob's face. Was it concern? Fear?

Miss Kate went back to pacing around the circle, making eye contact with each student as she spoke. "Sometimes hearing the Holy Spirit when he speaks is hard because he doesn't often speak with words we can hear with our ears—he usually speaks right into our minds or hearts, giving us a strong feeling about something he wants us to know. Other times, he prompts people in our lives to give us encouragement. Amazing, don't you think?" She paused to take another sip from her huge purple mug.

"The Holy Spirit also fills us up with the love of God! We can know lots of information *about* God in our minds, but the Holy Spirit is the one who makes God's love feel alive. I'd say he's super encouraging, wouldn't you?"

Miss Kate ducked behind her desk and pulled out a tall glass of milk. Lexi wondered what was going on—did she suddenly need a milk break? The rest of the faces in the circle reflected Lexi's confusion.

"Think of the Holy Spirit like this," Miss Kate said. "Let's say you want some chocolate milk, so you fill a glass with milk and squirt in some chocolate syrup."

Miss Kate reached back under the desk, pulled out a bottle of Hershey's syrup, and squirted some into the milk. Lexi's mouth began to water.

"Technically, we have chocolate milk now, right? But if you were to take a drink at this point, the milk probably wouldn't be very tasty. Why? Because the chocolate hasn't been stirred up yet! Once you grab a spoon and stir the chocolate into the milk, the chocolate takes over and makes the milk much more delicious."

She picked up a spoon from the desk and gave the milk a good stir. The chocolate clouded up from the bottom and mixed nicely into the formerly white milk.

Miss Kate took a big drink. "Ah! So much yummier than plain milk," she declared with a satisfied smile. "You see, when we become Christians, the Holy Spirit lives inside us, sort of like we're the milk and he's the chocolate syrup. But the chocolate syrup, or Holy Spirit, will just stay put at the bottom unless we make the choice to stir him up."

Lexi was intrigued by the chocolate milk analogy. The Holy Spirit was starting to make so much more sense.

"In other words," Miss Kate continued, "God wants the Holy Spirit to be active in the lives of all his followers, but he ultimately lets us choose how much we allow the Spirit to be a part of our lives. All we have to do is simply invite him to be active!" She paused, then asked, "Does this make sense? Isn't this kind of exciting? Is anyone else thirsty for chocolate milk now?" She grinned.

A mixture of smiles, nods, and cheers rippled throughout the room. Miss Kate sent Sam to get the jug of milk from the refrigerator in the next room, then passed out red plastic cups and spoons. Sam swiftly returned and soon everyone was stirring up their chocolate milk while Miss Kate passed out graham crackers to complete the snack. Lexi glanced at Millie who had a look of pure delight on her face. Lexi knew graham crackers and milk were one of her sister's favorite combinations, and a rare treat since their mother preferred stocking the fridge at home with cashew milk.

"Let's not forget the homework assignment!" Miss Kate clapped her hands with what Lexi decided was a little too much enthusiasm.

Lexi noticed there weren't quite as many groans from the students this week. She leaned in to listen to the assignment, careful not to tip over her milk. This Holy Spirit stuff was kind of fascinating, and she didn't want to miss the instructions.

Miss Kate cleared her throat and waited until the classroom was quiet before she began. "There are two ways to do the homework this week, and I want you to pick at least one. The first is to simply find someone who needs encouragement and ask the Holy Spirit to help you encourage them. The second is to notice how the Holy Spirit encourages *you* this week. And, if you're up for more of a challenge, try this—find a time when you're alone and can focus for a few minutes, then simply ask the Holy Spirit to encourage you and listen closely to what he says. Understand?"

Heads nodded all around the room.

"Great!" said Miss Kate. "I can't wait until next Sunday to hear how things go!"

CHAPTER 10

"Where do you kids want to go for lunch today?" Mr. Hanson asked as they crossed the busy church parking lot. Lexi, Sam, and Millie glanced back and forth as if reading each other's minds.

"Cracker Barrel!" they joyfully yelled in unison.

Mrs. Hanson laughed. "I don't know why you even bother to ask anymore, Jordan."

"I don't either," he replied, "but I'm not complaining. These kids have good taste—and I, for one, am looking forward to some roast beef and biscuits."

When they arrived at Cracker Barrel, Mr. Hanson had to circle the parking lot twice before he found an empty spot. After a fifteen-minute wait, which Lexi didn't mind since she enjoyed browsing the attached country store, they were seated at a spacious table next to a window.

"How was church this morning, kids?" Their mom slid her large purse under her chair, then sat up and eyed each of them in turn, awaiting responses.

Millie proudly showed her parents the rainbow notebook she had chosen from the prize box. Sam pulled a small, blue race car out of his jeans pocket to show off his prize as well.

Lexi didn't think any of them had mentioned last week's homework to their parents, or even talked much about what Miss Kate was teaching them. She wondered what her parents would think.

"What did you do to earn a prize today?" asked their dad. "Memorize a Bible verse?"

"Nope, we helped the Holy Spirit!" said Millie. "Or the Holy Spirit helped us. I'm not really sure ... but I helped Lexi do her chores, and Miss Kate was proud of me!" She sat up taller in her seat. Mr. and Mrs. Hanson looked surprised.

Sam tried to clarify. "Well, we were supposed to let the Holy Spirit help us last week. So I didn't wake you up when I had a bad dream!"

Mr. and Mrs. Hanson looked pleased, but their faces showed they were still a bit puzzled.

Lexi stepped in to explain. "What they're trying to say is last week we learned the Holy Spirit is the part of God who lives in us, and he can help us sometimes, like give us courage to do the right thing or help us feel better when we're scared—stuff like that. Miss Kate wanted us to let the Holy Spirit help us with something last week, so we did. And we got to pick out a prize after we shared our stories with the class."

Mr. and Mrs. Hanson stared at their three kids. Lexi could tell they weren't quite sure what to say.

Mrs. Hanson spoke first. "Wow, you guys! I'm really proud of you!" She met eyes with their dad, then continued. "Just so you know, this is pretty different than what Dad and I learned in Sunday school when we were growing up."

To Lexi, it looked as though her parents were having an entire conversation with each other, using only their eyes. She'd seen them communicate this way before and always wished they'd let her in on whatever it was they were saying.

After a brief pause, Mr. Hanson spoke up. "I think I may give Miss Kate a quick phone call later, so I can find out what exactly she's teaching you. I don't necessarily think she's teaching you anything wrong—this is just new to us, and we want to fully understand."

Lexi sighed. *Dad is going to call our teacher? How embarrassing.*

Her mom nodded in agreement. "We're so happy to see you guys enjoying church and even thinking about what you've learned during the week. Miss Kate must really be making the Bible come alive for you kids!"

Lexi couldn't help but smile. They had no idea. And even if her dad calling the teacher was a little embarrassing, Lexi supposed it would be good for her parents to learn about all this for themselves. Hopefully, they would understand and wouldn't think anything was too strange.

A friendly waitress with a thick, Southern accent interrupted. "Have you folks decided on your order yet?"

Lexi ordered her usual chicken-fried steak with sides of corn and fried okra, which her friends couldn't believe she liked, then turned her attention to the triangle peg game. An identical game sat in the center of each table in the restaurant, and her goal was always to beat her little brother. He usually won, so this time she was determined.

After Sam won the peg game twice, and Lexi finally beat him once, their food arrived. Mr. Hanson said grace while delicious aromas wafted from all sides of the table. Usually Lexi was too distracted to really listen to her father's prayer when they were at a restaurant, but this time was different for some reason.

"Amen," she said, wholeheartedly, when her father finished.

Lexi spent the afternoon pouring over the rest of her library books on the Revolutionary War. King George III, George Washington, Thomas Jefferson, Thomas Paine—so many Georges and Thomases. So many names, places, and dates, all swirling together in her brain like the little dust tornadoes she'd seen coming across the field near her grandparents' house, picking up old corn husks and debris as they went. That's how she felt. A little bit of school, a little bit of church, and a million other random thoughts, all fighting for her attention.

She closed her book. There was no point to studying in her current frame of mind. She squeezed her eyes shut, frustrated with herself for not being able to focus on history. If she wanted the trip, she had to focus. There was no real choice, considering three whole days at Six Flags was at stake—with friends, good food, and a hotel! She so badly wanted to go.

Lexi opened her eyes and her book, then shut her eyes tightly again. *Holy Spirit, I really need to focus on history right now. If you don't mind, will you help me? Please? And encourage me? I'm just not sure I can do it.*

Lexi hopped up and did a few jumping jacks, then ran in place for a minute, shaking her head back and forth. Taking a deep breath, she grabbed her history book from the bed and plopped down at her little desk.

New motivation struck. Lexi opened her pencil box and reached in. Looking at the pencil her fingers landed on, she realized it was one she'd picked from the church's prize box a few months ago. In her hand was a neon green pencil with the words "I can do all things through Christ who strengthens me" stamped down the side in bold, black letters.

Since that evening was their traditional Sunday free-for-all supper, Lexi wandered around the kitchen filling her plate with whatever looked good.

She walked into the living room, her plate full of apple slices, an empty tortilla, a handful of Craisins, and a leftover plain hot dog. She ignored her mother's raised eyebrows and amused expression as she watched her daughter walk past and take a seat on the couch. Lexi set her plate on the coffee table to wait for the rest of the family, hoping for something interesting on the nature show.

"How's your history assignment coming, dear?"

"Better than I thought it might," Lexi answered her mom honestly. "There's a lot to do, but I really, *really* want to go to Six Flags."

"I know you do, sweetie. And I know you've never cared much for history, but I do hope you'll finally see the value in knowing your history, once this is all said and done."

Lexi chuckled through a grimace. "I hope so too, Mom."

Mr. Hanson joined the rest of the family in the living room. "Well, I just got off the phone with Miss Kate."

Lexi's ears perked up.

"We had a good talk," Mr. Hanson continued. Lexi breathed a sigh of relief. "She told me about what you've been discussing in class, answered my questions, and explained everything very well. This is still a new idea to your mother and me—the Holy Spirit being such an active part of life—but I now see what you're being taught is true and biblical. To tell you the truth, we're looking forward to learning more ourselves."

Sam spoke up. "It's kind of weird for us kids to be learning about something you guys didn't even know, huh? I thought you knew everything—guess not!" He had an ornery gleam in his eyes.

Mr. and Mrs. Hanson laughed, then threatened Sam with a tickle fight if he didn't pipe down.

Giggling, Millie immediately hopped up and began tickling whoever she could reach, sparking a family-wide tickle fight, which lasted until Sam finally had enough and shouted, "Serious!" *Serious* was the family's code word for *stop tickling me!* It was a family rule that must be obeyed.

Everyone settled down, though Millie snuck in one last tickle before returning to the couch. Trying not to laugh, Sam shot her an annoyed look, while their dad cued up the nature show. The laughter faded, and Lexi and her family ate their unusual suppers as they learned every detail about Wisconsin river otters.

CHAPTER 11

Lexi dragged herself out of bed and washed her face in an attempt to wake up. The weekend had flown by, but excitement quickly started building for the week ahead. Sure, she had a math test coming up and a mountain of history assignments she needed to ace, but she was looking forward to the church homework of finding ways to encourage other people. She figured her friends would be a good place to start.

After settling on the third outfit she tried on and leaving the first and second outfits slung across her bed, Lexi galloped downstairs for breakfast. She devoured two pumpkin pancakes with extra syrup, then grabbed an apple and checked the clock. The bus would arrive in exactly seven minutes, allowing just enough time to brush her teeth, find her backpack, and kiss her mom goodbye. Her dad was already at work.

The bus came right on time, and Lexi and her siblings piled on. When they arrived at school, Lexi found Eliza and Claire talking in the hallway by their lockers. Lexi immediately noticed Claire's red-rimmed eyes and pursed lips. She was obviously holding back tears. Just as Lexi opened her mouth to ask what was wrong, the bell rang, and students began scrambling to their classrooms. Lexi would have to wait until recess to find out what was wrong.

Lexi was anxious to find out why Claire was so upset. Science class seemed to drag on forever, but just as she was beginning to think recess would never come, the bell rang, signaling twenty minutes of fresh air and freedom. Lexi usually didn't like the fifth and sixth graders having such an early recess—she wished it could be after lunch, when concentrating on schoolwork was harder—but that day she welcomed the piercing ring of the recess bell. She jumped from her seat and dashed outside to meet up with her friends near the monkey bars.

Claire seemed to have gained control of her emotions over the course of the morning. Her eyes were no longer red from holding back tears, but her usual smile was missing. Lexi was the only one who didn't know why Claire was upset. She asked gently, "Claire, what's wrong? Did something happen?"

Claire looked down and nodded. "My dad's moving out. My parents just told me last night. I mean, I knew they argued all the time, but I didn't expect *this* to happen! I don't know what's going to happen now. I think he'll still live here in town somewhere, but I don't know how often I'll get to see him or anything." Claire clenched her teeth together, and Lexi could tell she was doing her best to keep from bursting into tears.

Eliza spoke up, "I'm so sorry, Claire. This is just awful. But who knows—maybe they'll work things out!"

Lexi wasn't quite sure what to say. She honestly couldn't imagine the feeling of having her parents separate. She only knew it would be terrible, and Claire must feel completely helpless.

Abruptly, Lexi thought of the Holy Spirit. *What did Miss Kate say about him again? Oh, yeah—that he's the most encouraging encourager of all.* Lexi silently said a quick prayer for the Holy Spirit to help as she tried to encourage her friend.

Lexi reached out to give her friend's hand a reassuring squeeze. "I'm so sorry, Claire. I know I can't possibly understand what you're going through right now, but you're my friend and I'm here for you—if you ever need to talk or cry, or just hang out after school so you can be distracted for a little while … anything at all. You're strong, and I know you'll get through this. And you're not alone!" She glanced at Eliza. "We're here to help, right?"

Eliza quickly nodded in agreement and reached out to rub Claire's shoulder, reinforcing Lexi's message.

Claire wrapped her arms around Lexi and Eliza for a group hug. "Thanks, Lexi," she whispered. "I don't know what I'd do without you guys." She smiled weakly at Eliza. "For some reason, I feel a lot more peaceful right now than I have since I got the terrible news last night." She inhaled deeply. "You guys are the best."

Lexi considered telling Claire about the Holy Spirit but wasn't sure this was the right time. She knew Claire went to church with her mom once in a while, but she had never thought to talk to her about God. She was pretty sure the Holy Spirit was just another name in the Bible as far as Claire was concerned. For that matter, he was only a name in the Bible to Lexi not even two weeks ago.

Lexi could hardly believe she had only known about the Holy Spirit for such a short time. To her surprise, she realized knowing him had completely changed the way she thought lately.

Over the past week or so, she had found herself being more patient and understanding with the people around her. She wanted her friends to experience this change too, but although she wasn't exactly afraid to talk to them about the Holy Spirit, she had a feeling they weren't quite ready to understand. Not yet, anyway.

Lexi decided to pray for the words to talk to her friends when the time was right. She had an unexplainable new confidence in the Holy Spirit. The bell rang, warning the students that classes would resume in five minutes, and the noisy bunch of fifth and sixth graders headed back into the school.

Lexi and Claire had art next. They walked to class together in silence, Lexi trying her best to focus on the rest of the school day.

As soon as Mrs. Clark, the art teacher, took her usual position at the front of the class and began to speak, Lexi pulled a small piece of paper from her notebook and wrote a quick note—

"Claire, would you come to church with me and my family next Sunday? We have a really nice teacher. I think you'd like her."

Lexi folded the paper into a small triangle, then doodled a tiny heart and smiley face next to Claire's name on the front. She smoothly slipped the note under Claire's sketch pad on the desk behind her, then waited.

Lexi heard the crinkle of paper as Claire unfolded the note as quietly as possible to avoid drawing Mrs. Clark's attention. A minute later, Lexi felt Claire gently tug a strand of her hair, so she reached her hand behind her and felt Claire place the note back into her hand. Lexi quietly unwrapped it under her desk.

Her face fell as she read Claire's response: "Not interested. Thanks anyway."

∾

The day dragged on until at last supper had been eaten, homework was finished, and the time had finally come for Lexi to crawl into her cozy bed where she could think without distractions (namely, Sam and Millie).

Sunday was just yesterday—how could it already feel so far away? She had tried to do the church homework of letting the Holy Spirit use her to encourage somebody. She felt like the Holy Spirit *had* used her to encourage Claire when they were on the playground, but she was disappointed Claire rejected her offer to come to church with them.

Claire could have written back something like, *I can't, I'm busy that morning,* or *it's just not going to work for me this week,* but she hadn't. She had simply written *not interested.*

Lexi tried not to be discouraged. She knew Claire was going through a lot with her dad moving out, so she did her best not to take the rejection personally. If only Claire could know what Lexi knew. If only she could know for herself the life-changing effects of having the Holy Spirit live inside her, giving her peace and guiding her through each day.

"God," Lexi whispered into the dark, "please help my friend Claire know you better. She really needs your help. Amen."

CHAPTER 12

Relieved to have another week of school behind her, Lexi collapsed onto her bed and reached for her library book. Only four more weeks until summer break (not that she was counting). She had paid close attention in history class and was surprised to notice the lessons weren't quite as boring as they used to be. In fact, some of the stories were halfway interesting. Amazingly, she seemed to be learning a lot, which her parents would be happy to hear.

Lexi had turned her report in to Mr. Drye first thing that morning. She was excited to have a report-free weekend ahead of her, but was anxious to get her grade back on Monday. Although she felt pretty good about what she had written, she was still afraid she'd missed something important or done something wrong. Already receiving As on all her new classroom assignments meant the Revolutionary War report was the only thing standing between her and Six Flags.

Overhearing her brother and sister's shouts and laughter, Lexi looked up from her book. She could tell from snippets of conversation she overheard that they were in Millie's room playing Memory, a game Sam always won. He was so good at Memory, their mother sometimes refused to play because she was tired of losing so badly. Sam found it hilarious. Lexi was sure Sam had chosen this game now, knowing he would beat his little sister.

Sam's voice traveled down the hallway. "You can do it, Millie! Think hard. Remember which one I picked up last time?"

Lexi's jaw dropped at hearing such encouraging words come from her little brother's mouth during a board game. After a brief pause, she heard Millie shouting, "I did it! I got a match, all by myself!"

The next thing she knew, Millie was rushing into Lexi's room to share the news. "Lexi, I finally, *finally*, got a match! I did it!" Millie threw her arms around Lexi in celebration, then exited as quickly as she had entered.

Lexi smiled as she overheard her brother and sister from her room at the end of the hall. "I knew you could do it!" Sam said, celebrating with Millie.

Now she was sure this was Sam's attempt at completing his church homework. Even though she had to admit Sam was a pretty good brother, she knew how competitive he was at games and how unusual it was for him to encourage anyone who might end up beating him.

Lexi grinned, proud of her brother. *Well, he finished his homework with almost two days to spare.*

§

After supper that evening, Lexi's family sprawled throughout the living room, each with their attention turned to different activities. Lexi was working on her new extreme dot-to-dot book, Sam and Millie were watching cartoons on TV, her dad was in the recliner working on the laptop, and her mother was making a grocery list for the next week. (Earlier that day, Lexi had sneaked *donuts* onto the list, hoping the handwriting would look like her dad's, so her mom might actually buy them.)

Lexi glanced at her dad. His brow was furrowed as he stared hard at the computer screen. She overheard her mom ask him what was wrong, and he answered something about work that Lexi didn't understand. It sounded complicated.

Millie was at her father's side in an instant. She quietly slid onto his lap, careful not to bump the computer. "I love you, Daddy," she said, her big, blue eyes gazing up at him. "You're the best daddy ever." She gave him a big hug and a kiss on each cheek before she hopped down and rejoined Sam on the floor to finish watching the show.

When Lexi glanced back at her parents, she immediately noticed the shift in her father's demeanor. She could tell he was holding back happy tears. The stress of work seemed to melt away in light of his younger daughter's encouragement, at least for the moment.

Lexi watched as her parents' eyes met. They shared a smile and a quick kiss before returning to their previous tasks. Lexi knew her dad must still have a work problem to figure out, but the worry that controlled his face just thirty seconds ago had been replaced with peace.

CHAPTER 13

"Breakfast time!"

As soon as Lexi heard her father calling from downstairs, she quickly finished brushing her hair and raced down to the breakfast table. She loved her dad's Sunday morning breakfasts. Her mom was responsible for breakfast the rest of the week, but she usually stuck with simple eggs or cereal. Her dad, on the other hand, liked to create more complicated dishes.

Lexi arrived in the kitchen to find a stack of homemade bacon-egg-and-cheese breakfast sandwiches awaiting the family. She gave her dad a quick hug of thanks and took a seat.

After everyone was seated and grace had been said, Lexi's mom glanced around the table. "Are you kids looking forward to church this morning?"

Sam gave an affirmative grunt, his half-chewed breakfast sandwich nearly falling out of his mouth.

"Yep!" answered Lexi, washing down her bite with a sip of water.

Millie nodded enthusiastically as she chewed, swallowed, and smiled her big cheesy grin.

Lexi used to think Millie's big smiles and happy outlook on life were fake, sort of like a show she put on without really trying. Over time, she realized Millie truly *was* as happy as she seemed. Usually, that is.

Sometimes Lexi wished some of Millie's innate happiness would rub off on her. A lot more effort was required of Lexi to look on the bright side of things, although she did try. Lexi smiled to herself with pleasant surprise, as she realized looking on the bright side seemed to be getting a little easier lately.

"We need to leave in ten minutes," Mr. Hanson announced, before draining the last drops from his coffee mug. "Everybody brush your teeth, use the bathroom, and get your shoes on!"

After clearing the breakfast dishes in a hurry, they did as they were told. To their mother's astonishment, ten minutes later they were all buckled in the SUV, ready for church.

"Well, this is a welcome surprise," Mrs. Hanson said, laughing. "Everyone found their shoes and everything. We might even be early for once—imagine that!"

As Mr. Hanson backed out of the driveway, Lexi overheard her little sister whisper to Sam in the backseat, "Don't tell Mommy I didn't brush my teeth!"

Lexi wasn't the only one who overheard. In a flash, their mother passed back a stick of peppermint gum. "Millie, chew this until we get to church. And next time brush your teeth like you're told. No more being sneaky to get out of it, do you understand?"

"Yes, Mommy." Millie frowned. Lexi knew her little sister loved gum, but truly hated peppermint.

Mrs. Hanson joked that she might faint from joy when they arrived at church early. Lexi, Sam, and Millie couldn't help but laugh at their parents when their father got in place behind his wife, as if ready to catch her.

After getting checked in, Lexi, Sam, and Millie made their way down the colorful hallway to their classroom, saying *hi* to Mandy and some other volunteers as they passed.

Miss Kate was the only one inside when they reached the classroom. "Good morning!" she greeted them, looking up from a stack of papers and offering a warm smile. "Go ahead and play with the toys or puzzles until the rest of the class arrives." She sipped her coffee, then turned to finish reviewing her notes.

Lexi, Sam, and Millie worked together on a hundred-piece jungle puzzle as the other children filtered in. Just before the last monkey was complete, everyone had arrived, and Miss Kate called out to gather them for class.

The students took their seats in the circle. As they gave Miss Kate their full attention, Lexi realized she must not be the only one who had begun looking forward to church. She glanced around at the (mostly) eager faces and smiled to herself, remembering the dread she felt on the first day of this new class.

"Good morning!" Miss Kate began, her typical broad smile filling her face. "I'm so glad you're all here this morning. Any volunteers who want to share how they worked with the Holy Spirit to encourage someone this past week?"

Sam's hand shot up first, which took Lexi by surprise since her little brother was usually pretty reserved in class. She leaned back in her chair, ready to hear Sam tell his story of how he encouraged Millie during their game of Memory.

"I was at lunch in school last week," began Sam.

Lexi sat up straight, her eyes staring at her brother as he spoke. *Wait a minute—lunch? What on earth is he talking about?*

Sam continued, "And a kid in my class, Kyle, sneaked two cartons of chocolate milk when he was supposed to just take one. He sat by me, and when I noticed, he told me not to tell. I said he should take one of them back and tell the lunch lady the truth. I told him my mom always says when you do something wrong, you should tell the truth because you'll be in less trouble if you tell the truth than if you lie and get caught."

Sam focused his eyes on a long, black scuff mark on the white tile floor while he spoke. "At first Kyle didn't want to tell the truth because he was scared he'd get in trouble, but I told him he should anyway. He finally took the milk back, apologized, and didn't even get in trouble! He said he thought it was funny at first, but then started feeling guilty, and he was *glad* I told him to return it. Anyway, I think maybe the Holy Spirit helped me, because I usually wouldn't have said anything at all, but this time I knew it would be wrong not to."

Miss Kate praised him, "Well done, Sam! The Holy Spirit really helped you encourage your friend to do the right thing!"

Lexi looked at her little brother, completely taken by surprise. She'd been sure Sam's story was going to be about the time he encouraged Millie during their game. That was a completely new side of "game-playing" Sam, and she had assumed he was putting a lot of effort into encouraging Millie so he could get his church homework done.

But she was wrong—evidently all they'd been learning in class was really starting to soak in, even for her seven-year-old brother. Lexi caught Sam's eye and gave him a smile with a quick thumbs up. He grinned back, clearly happy to have pleased his big sister.

A few more students shared their stories, but Lexi noticed Jacob remained silent. She was sure he hadn't tried the homework this time. It was too bad he was so discouraged after his attempt last week.

Lexi volunteered to go next.

"This week, I found out one of my friends is going through something really hard at home. It's really sad for her, and she was pretty upset at school. I feel like the Holy Spirit helped me know the right things to say to encourage her." Lexi twisted her blue ring round and round her finger, a nervous habit she picked up a few months ago.

"Usually I would've said something like 'It'll be okay' or 'I'm sorry you're sad,' but this time I had more to say, and it seemed to hit home with her and make her feel better. I was so glad to have helped her feel a little better."

Lexi looked up and saw Miss Kate smiling down. "That's excellent, Lexi! I bet your friend appreciated your encouraging words more than you know."

Miss Kate looked out over the classroom. "Is there anyone else who wants to share their story with us? Millie?"

Lexi's eyes landed on Millie, who was picking at her fingernails with an uncharacteristic serious expression on her face.

"I accidentally forgot about the homework," Millie admitted in a voice that could barely be heard, a look of dejection seeming to consume her whole body. Lexi thought she saw tears starting to form.

Miss Kate assured her she needn't worry and was about to continue with class when Lexi spoke up. "Wait! Millie *did* do the homework!" Lexi almost shouted, lunging forward in her seat so abruptly she almost fell off the edge. Millie looked up with surprise and confusion, waiting for Lexi to continue.

"A few days ago, our dad was really stressed about some work thing on the computer, so Millie jumped into his lap and told him what a good dad he is. She gave him a big hug and went back to playing, so she couldn't see his face, but I did. He looked really worried before she encouraged him, but afterwards he looked so much happier!" Lexi glanced at Millie and saw a smile coming back to her sister's face, her eyes shining as she remembered the evening Lexi described.

"Thank you for speaking up, Lexi. And I'm very proud of you, Millie," Miss Kate said gently. "You're one of the youngest here, and I understand if you have trouble remembering the homework. What makes me so happy is that you didn't even *realize* you were encouraging your dad, which means you've already started letting the Holy Spirit live through you naturally. That's pretty impressive, especially when you're five years old. There are lots of grown-ups who can't even do that yet."

Millie jumped up and ran straight to Miss Kate, silently giving her a big hug before running back to her seat.

"Go ahead and get the prize box, Millie," said Miss Kate with a warm chuckle. "You can be the first to choose a prize, then you can pass the box around."

Positively glowing, Millie popped back up from her seat and walked quickly across the room to retrieve the green treasure chest from the shelf. As she passed Lexi, she slowed her pace just enough to lean down and whisper in Lexi's ear, "Thanks, Sis."

After the prize box circulated (Lexi chose a light-yellow bracelet in the shape of a heart), Miss Kate was ready to begin the new lesson.

CHAPTER 14

Miss Kate cleared her throat and stepped inside the circle of folding chairs. "You may have noticed our previous lessons sort of overlap. What I mean is, sometimes it's hard to know if the Holy Spirit is helping or if he's encouraging. He sometimes does both at the same time, don't you think?"

Miss Kate took a long drink from her travel mug before continuing. Lexi could smell the coffee steaming from the top. Lexi loved the smell of coffee—the aroma reminded her of peaceful early mornings at home with her mom and dad. But even though she liked the smell, she hated the taste. She had discovered this one morning when she was seven, after her dad offered her a sip. The black coffee was so gross she had actually spit it onto the floor.

Miss Kate placed her mug back on the desk. "Today, we're going to learn some ways the Holy Spirit speaks to us. Of course, he speaks to us in our hearts and minds as we've already seen, but he doesn't stop there. Sometimes he speaks to us a little more directly."

Lexi wasn't sure what Miss Kate was getting at, but she was done assuming she knew all there was to know about God and was eager to keep learning. This was different from simply learning Bible stories, not that there was anything wrong with Bible stories. She knew those were helpful too, but this was real, live stuff she could use in everyday life.

"Sometimes," Miss Kate continued, "when you quiet your heart and mind and listen for the Holy Spirit, he will tell you things. Things about another person you couldn't have otherwise known, so you can pray for and encourage the person."

Lexi was confused. *Like fortune telling? Isn't that supposed to be a bad thing?*

"For example," said Miss Kate, "I may have a sick friend and want to say a prayer for him. When I'm *not* deliberately listening to the Holy Spirit,

I would probably say a perfectly nice prayer such as, 'God, please heal my friend. Help the sickness go away so he can feel better.' You don't have to know any special details to pray like that, right? And is this kind of prayer good?" She stopped to wait for the children's nods. "Absolutely!"

"But if I *am* deliberately listening to the Holy Spirit, I may say something more like ..." Miss Kate closed her eyes, and for a second, Lexi thought she was really praying for someone. "God, please heal my friend. He's sick, and I'm sensing from you he's scared he'll end up having cancer like his mother. Replace his fear with peace. Heal his body and calm his mind. In Jesus's name. Amen." Miss Kate opened her eyes and looked around the room. "Do you see the difference?"

Many heads nodded while others simply stared, trying to understand.

Okay, not quite like fortune telling ... but still a little weird. Lexi's eyes narrowed in concentration as she thought through all Miss Kate was saying.

"I wouldn't have known before I began to pray that my friend's mother had cancer or that he was afraid he had it too. But if the Holy Spirit gives me details like these, I can pray more specifically and possibly more effectively."

Miss Kate continued to speak intently as she rose from her seat and walked around the circle in long, slow strides. "Listening to the Holy Spirit like this allows me to encourage my friend by sharing the message with him. His faith might even be strengthened, knowing God is speaking to others on his behalf!"

Lexi was amazed at the thought of the Holy Spirit telling her something she otherwise never would have known. *Seriously, is this for real?*

"That's one way the Holy Spirit might speak to us. We won't stop there, though. Sometimes, the Holy Spirit puts words or pictures in our minds as a direct message for another person, or even for ourselves—we call these *words of knowledge*, or simply *words*.

"These words or pictures may not make any sense to us, but if we share them with the person God intends, they could end up meaning something very powerful. I know this may be difficult to understand at first, so let me give you some examples."

The sound of Miss Kate's low brown boots echoed throughout the large room as she paced back and forth on the tile floor. Lexi was reminded of the sound her art teacher, Mrs. Clark, made when she walked down the long school hallway.

"Let's say I'm praying for my friend, when suddenly the words *right now* pop into my head. Now, I wasn't thinking those words all by myself because they honestly make no sense to me, but if I go to my friend and tell him I felt the Holy Spirit gave me the words *right now* to share with him, it may mean something very important to him.

"To him, the words could mean he should take the job he wasn't sure he should take. Or they might mean he should sign up to be his son's Cub Scouts leader like he'd been thinking about for months. The course of his life could ultimately be changed—isn't that powerful?" Miss Kate gave an incredulous smile, as half the students stared with wide eyes and the other half fidgeted in their seats, ready for the approaching snack time.

"Now I want to give you an example of a time when God might put a picture in our minds. The idea is the same as what we just talked about, except using a picture instead of words.

Miss Kate nodded at Sam. "Let's pretend Sam here is praying for his friend. Let's call his friend … George."

Sam smiled.

Miss Kate continued, "Now let's say a picture of a fishing boat pops into Sam's mind, and he feels like the Holy Spirit wants him to share the image with George and tell him God loves him. Sam can't make any sense of the image—for all he knows George has never been fishing in his life." Sam's smile widened at the thought.

"Imagine Sam is obedient to the Holy Spirit and tells George about the fishing boat image. George may tell Sam that his grandfather used to take him out on the lake in a fishing boat every summer before he moved into a nursing home last year. Maybe this was the first summer in his life George's grandpa wasn't able to take him fishing, and it was really sad for him. Maybe because Sam shared this image, George ends up knowing God loves him and wants to comfort him."

Miss Kate spread her arms wide. "Wouldn't it be awesome to be a part of bringing God's love to someone like that?" She paused to flip through her fat, leather-bound Bible.

Lexi liked the idea of bringing God's love to others in such a powerful way, but she was a little unsure. Was this stuff even in the Bible? She didn't remember ever hearing these ideas before now.

Miss Kate found the spot she was looking for. "In 1 Corinthians 12:8, the apostle Paul says, 'To one person the Spirit gives the ability to give wise advice; to another the same Spirit gives a message of special knowledge.'"

Well I guess that explains that. Lexi was relieved to learn this new lesson was, in fact, biblical.

Miss Kate went on, "Now, there's no guarantee the Spirit will give you a message of special knowledge every time you ask for one, so don't be discouraged if that's the case, but from my experience, he often does give them to those who believe, ask, and listen."

Lexi's head was swimming from the exciting new ideas. In her old class, Lexi would have begun planning out her Cracker Barrel order in her mind at this point, but not today.

"Here's another thing to consider," Miss Kate said, closing her Bible and returning the thick book to her desk. "Often after we share a word with another person, we have a chance to pray for that person right then and there. There are lots of people with good intentions who will tell you 'I'll be praying for you' or 'You're in my prayers.' There's certainly nothing wrong with that approach, but think about this for a moment—how much more powerful might it be to pray for the person face-to-face and see what God wants to do through your prayer in that very moment? Even if we don't exactly understand why, God clearly likes when we work together in prayer."

Miss Kate moved her glasses to the top of her head and returned to her seat on the tall stool. Lexi was glad. She was starting to get dizzy watching Miss Kate pace.

"Sometimes people get nervous, but from what I've seen, it's quite rare for a person to tell you no when you ask if you can pray for them, whether they're a Christian or not. So the good news is there's really not much to be nervous about!" Miss Kate shared an encouraging smile.

"In fact, I have seven short words I want you to remember. These words are extremely powerful and have the potential to change the world," she went on, dramatically. "They are adventurous and faith-building words, and I want you to repeat them after me."

Lexi and a few other older students exchanged baffled glances as they tried to think what the seven words could possibly be. The rest of the class looked on, waiting.

"Are you ready?" asked Miss Kate. "Okay, here we go … 'Can. I. pray. for. you. right. now?'" Miss Kate spoke each word clearly and separately.

The class repeated the words together. Lexi felt herself growing nervous. She couldn't remember the last time she prayed for someone out loud and in person. To be honest, she wasn't sure she ever had.

Miss Kate continued, "We've mostly talked about listening to the Holy Spirit when we're praying for others, but the Holy Spirit also has things he wants to say just to you! All we have to do is take the time to ask and listen." She stopped and looked around the room at the expressive faces looking back at her.

"I can tell this is hard for some of you to believe, but we'll finish up soon, and I would love to answer any questions after class." She stood again. Lexi hoped she wouldn't resume her pacing.

"Now, I want to be honest and make sure you know this isn't always easy. Sometimes, the Holy Spirit's voice is hard to hear. Sometimes, we think we hear him but when we share the message with the person it was for, that person doesn't think it relates to them at all. And you know what? That's okay!" she declared, answering her own question.

"The important part is our obedience. Sometimes, that's God's whole plan all along. He'll use these opportunities, whether we're spot on or not, to help us grow into braver, more powerful children of God."

Lexi had to admit she felt relieved to hear she wasn't expected to be great at this right away. Or possibly ever.

"There's one more point I want to make before we finish up. Are any of you involved in sports or music?" Almost everyone nodded as Miss Kate scanned the room. "Then you probably already know in order to do your best at something, you need to practice. Practice makes your muscles stronger and your mind sharper, so you get better and better." She glanced around with enthusiasm.

"Your spirituality is just like a muscle! The more you try listening to the Holy Spirit, the easier it will get to hear him. Soon, you'll discover hearing him doesn't take as much effort anymore!"

Lexi hoped what Miss Kate said was true, but it sure was hard to imagine that hearing the Holy Spirit would ever come naturally.

"Now for today's homework." Most of the class looked hesitantly at Miss Kate, although there weren't as many groans as last week. "The homework is simple," she said. The students breathed a collective sigh of relief.

"Simple, but not necessarily easy," she went on with a smile, as the class immediately went from relief to uncertainty again.

"This week, I simply want you to practice listening to the Holy Spirit. Try asking him if he has anything to tell you, quiet yourself enough to listen, and then obey what he asks of you. Ask. Listen. Obey. Can you remember that?"

The students nodded in unison.

"Good. And remember, there's no right or wrong way to do this as long as you ask, listen, and obey."

Lexi felt nervous but excited. The Holy Spirit being active and wanting to speak to her was still such a new idea. A pretty mind-blowing idea, to be honest.

Lexi noticed a mixture of expressions on the other kids' faces. Some were excited, some looked unsure, and one in particular looked almost annoyed.

Jacob.

Lexi felt bad for him. She knew he was discouraged after he gave the Holy Spirit a chance and felt he had been let down.

She said a silent prayer for Jacob to experience the Holy Spirit for himself.

෴

After church, Lexi's family headed straight to Cracker Barrel. Earlier in the week, everyone had readily agreed to Mr. Hanson's suggestion that the restaurant become their weekly Sunday lunch spot.

As Lexi half-listened to Sam and Millie tell their parents how church went that morning, she thought how different this week had been from a month ago. Back then, Cracker Barrel was the best part about Sundays. Lately, although she definitely looked forward to lunch, eating out after church was no longer the *only* thing she looked forward to on Sundays.

Learning about the Holy Spirit had unlocked a whole new world for her. Now, instead of being a place where she simply learned information about God, church had become a place where she could learn to be God's partner. She felt as though something inside her was waking up from a deep sleep, and now, every day seemed like an adventure. Nerves and excitement tingled as she wondered what this new week would hold.

POWER UP

Lexi exhaled contentedly as her dad pulled the car into the restaurant parking lot. Thankful for good food and fun with her family, Lexi was more than ready to give her mind a little rest. The thought of chicken-fried steak (or would she choose a bacon cheeseburger this time?) made her mouth begin to water, and she couldn't wait to beat her little brother at the triangle peg game. Or try, anyway.

CHAPTER 15

"What are you working on, sweetie?" Mrs. Hanson asked as she entered the kitchen late Sunday afternoon.

"Just finishing up a grammar worksheet I almost forgot about," Lexi answered.

While shuffling through her backpack to make sure every bit of schoolwork was finished for the next day, Lexi had discovered a single grammar worksheet at the bottom of her purple backpack, squashed under a heavy math book. She had quickly pulled out a pencil to complete the page before she forgot again.

Mrs. Hanson bustled around the kitchen, pulling out food options for their free-for-all supper. "Just so you know, Lexi, I'm really proud of you. You're so responsible about getting your homework done on time. I never have to worry about checking to make sure you've done it all. Well, unless you're falling asleep while studying history, that is," she added with a short laugh. "But I know you've been working extra hard to get that history grade up. Keep up the good work, sweetheart."

"Thanks, Mom. I'm not so sure about the church homework Miss Kate gave us today, though. It sounds kind of difficult."

"What?" Her mom raised her eyebrows. "I didn't realize she gave you more homework. What did she assign this week?"

"She wants us to ask the Holy Spirit if he has anything to tell us, listen to him, and then obey. Sounds simple enough, I guess, but the thought of actually *doing* it is a little scary. I don't want to mess up or hear something wrong, and it's not as if he'll write everything down on a nice little sticky note and hand it to me—I wish," she added, only half joking.

"Listen, Lex. I'm still new to this idea of the Holy Spirit speaking to us and being an active part of our lives, just like you are," her mom replied. "And I completely understand your fears. But the thing is, I've been following God long enough to have learned that fear is not something he wants for us. There's even a verse about it somewhere. In 2 Timothy maybe … hold on a sec while I check."

Lexi waited while her mom pulled her blue Bible from the small bookshelf next to the microwave. Lexi had noticed the Bible lying on the kitchen counter more frequently lately and knew her mom was using it quite a bit more these days.

Lexi thought it was great that her mom was getting into this Holy Spirit stuff—her dad was too, for that matter. Usually, her parents already knew everything, but this was something they could learn together, as a family. Lexi smiled as she waited for her mom to find the passage.

"Here!" Her mom squinted down at a page full of tiny print. "2 Timothy 1:7 says, 'For God has not given us a spirit of fear and timidity, but of power, love, and self-discipline.'

"In other words, Lexi, if you're feeling fearful about how it will go when you try listening to the Holy Spirit, that fear is *not* from God. He wants to help you be full of power and love instead. Does that make sense?"

Lexi nodded. She remembered hearing those words before. She thought the verse may have been printed on a little notebook she got from the prize box at church a few years ago. She wondered where the notebook ended up—probably stranded behind her bookcase or in some other place that rarely got cleaned. It was a good verse to remember, for sure.

"Thanks, Mom. That's actually pretty helpful."

"*Actually?*" her mom teased. "As if you're *surprised* I told you something helpful? Just for that, I'm giving you this for supper." She pulled some neglected celery from the back of the fridge and handed the floppy stalk to Lexi.

"Enjoy," she said with a smile and a wink, before heading into the living room to find the nature show for that evening.

Lexi laughed and shook her head, thinking about how goofy her parents could be. *Are other kids' parents like this? I doubt it.*

She sent the old celery down the garbage disposal before choosing something more appealing for supper. She decided lunchmeat, chips, and a banana would do just fine. After piling the items onto a plate, she carried her meal into the living room where the TV was already on, and the rest of her family sat waiting, ready to learn all about the lifecycle of tree frogs.

Later, in the darkness of bedtime, Lexi lay in bed, wide awake, thinking about the lesson from church that morning. She figured there was no time like the present to give the homework a try, so she closed her eyes and whispered into the dark, "Holy Spirit? Is there anything you want to tell me?"

Lexi waited, closing her eyes tightly and trying to rid her mind of the intrusive thoughts of her extra credit report, upcoming flute recital, and random conversations from earlier in the day.

This is going to be trickier than I thought.

She asked again. Waited again. Tried to clear her mind again. Why did her head keep filling up with other thoughts? Lexi said another prayer, asking God to help clear her mind since she apparently wasn't able to do so on her own.

After what seemed like forever, Lexi saw in her mind a beautiful, detailed picture of her house. She saw the cozy white Cape Cod-style home with the big maple trees in the yard and her loving family safe inside, and she felt thankful. Not just glad, but down-in-the-depths-of-her-soul thankful.

Lexi briefly wondered if her own mind was coming up with this scene or if the Holy Spirit brought the picture to mind. She decided it must be the work of the Holy Spirit. The image just wasn't something she would have thought up herself. Although she was glad to have her home and family, she didn't often stop to think how special they were or to feel so infinitely thankful. She knew the Holy Spirit was encouraging her to be thankful for all she had. She whispered a sincere thanks to God and allowed herself to drift off to sleep.

CHAPTER 16

Lexi awoke Monday morning to the obnoxious beeping of her alarm clock. After pressing the snooze button twice, she forced herself to roll out of her warm bed. The realization this was the day she'd get her history report back slammed to the front of her mind. She had felt pretty good about her work at first, but the longer she waited for her results, the more nervous she became. This would make or break her class trip. Talk about pressure.

After getting dressed and giving her hair a loose braid, Lexi meandered down to the kitchen, not really wanting the day to begin. As soon as she walked downstairs, the mouth-watering aroma of breakfast began changing her attitude about the day ahead.

Lexi's mom was standing by the stove, adding freshly cooked French toast to a growing pile, which she kept warm on a pizza pan in the oven. Like every weekday, her dad had already left for work.

French toast was Lexi's favorite. She took two slices from the oven and smothered them in butter and syrup just as her mom came over to kiss the top of her head.

"Morning, Mom. Thanks for the French toast. This smells awesome!" Lexi gave her a quick side-hug before digging in.

Lexi ate until she was full, then went upstairs to brush her teeth and grab her backpack. Lexi, Sam, and Millie hugged their mother goodbye before heading down the long driveway to meet the bus.

"Good luck on your history report, Lexi!" her mom called from the doorway as she waved goodbye.

"Thanks, Mom!" Lexi smiled, giving a small wave back as she climbed onto the bus.

The trip to school felt extra-long as Lexi sat wondering about her history grade. After the bus pulled into the parking lot, the students piled off in a mob and rushed to their classes. Lexi's mind turned to Miss Kate's homework assignment. She wasn't sure if she would do the homework today or just wait and see how the week went. Claire passed by, going the opposite direction in the hallway, and they shared smiles and a quick *hello* before continuing to their classrooms.

On her way to science class, Lexi stopped in front of a familiar classroom. She timidly peeked through the open door. "Mr. Drye?" Her voice echoed throughout the nearly empty room.

"Well, good morning, Lexi!" he answered. "Anxious for history to begin early today?" He chuckled at his own joke.

Lexi laughed politely and moved toward his desk. "I was just wondering if you graded my report yet. I can't wait to find out what I got." She held her breath, waiting for his reply.

Mr. Drye smiled. "I happen to have your report right here." He reached into the leather bag that sat on the floor near his chair and handed the papers to Lexi.

She looked down.

Staring straight up at her was a big, beautiful, red A+.

"Congratulations, Lexi! With the As you've been earning for the past two weeks on classroom assignments, and this excellent extra credit report, you've raised your overall classroom grade to a solid B+, just in time for it to count toward your trip."

Stunned, Lexi stared back at Mr. Drye. A smile slowly spread across her face as she realized what this meant.

She had raised her grade! She'd actually done it! Now the school would pay for her class trip, and she could really, truly go. The planning could officially begin—she'd have to talk with Claire and Eliza about what outfits they should pack and what snacks they'd all bring. They could create a shared playlist for their MP3 players, and maybe even go swimsuit shopping together!

Now that she was officially attending the trip, there were lots of details to think about and plan. She couldn't wait to tell Claire and Eliza. And her mom and dad—they'd be so proud of her!

"Thank you, Mr. Drye. Thank you so much!" she almost shouted, as she raced out the door, hurrying to science so she wouldn't be counted tardy.

POWER UP

"Don't thank me, Lexi," he called back, loudly enough for her to hear as she dashed around the corner. "You earned it!"

Lexi sat in science class trying to pay attention, but focusing on anything except the trip was difficult. She had poured herself into history over the past few weeks, and all that studying had finally paid off—she could hardly believe it. The Revolutionary War even made sense now (well, mostly), which she knew would make her parents happy. Just a few more weeks until she'd be in St. Louis, riding roller coasters with her friends. She thought she might explode from happiness any second.

For the remainder of class, Lexi forced herself to pay just enough attention to avoid the teacher suspecting her of daydreaming. After an exceptionally long hour, the bell rang, signaling recess—the one time of day Lexi was glad to hear the sound of the harsh, loud bell.

Lexi gathered her books and pencil and zipped them into her backpack. She decided she might as well use the two-minute walk outside to try listening for the Holy Spirit. Remembering the overwhelming feeling of thankfulness he had given her last night, she wondered what he might do if she asked again. Doing her best to quiet her mind, she expertly made her way through the busy school halls.

Unsure what to expect, she was taken by surprise when she immediately heard "Lexi, remember how much I love you," coming from a small voice somewhere deep in her mind.

She was amazed. Had God himself just spoken to her?

Seconds later, Claire popped into Lexi's thoughts, and she heard, "It's not your fault—trust me." *Sheesh, the Holy Spirit sure is moving fast this morning. He must know I only have two minutes.*

But then, Lexi stopped in her tracks. Was the Holy Spirit asking her to give this message to Claire? She sighed, already knowing the answer to her question. As awesome as it was to have the Holy Spirit *speak* to her, Lexi wasn't sure how much Claire would want to hear this message. If she clearly didn't want any part of going to church, why would she listen to anything Lexi had to tell her about God? If she got mad or thought Lexi was being pushy, what would that do to their friendship?

The church homework popped into her mind. *Ask, listen, obey.* Lexi had asked and listened—now, it was up to her whether she would obey.

Keeping the message to herself would definitely be easiest. That way no one would feel uncomfortable or nervous, like she was feeling now.

On the other hand, how would she feel if she decided *not* to obey? Guilty, probably. Lexi reached down, picked a tall dandelion puff, and blew. She stopped and watched the fluffy bits fly gently above the grass. She knew she needed to give Claire the message.

Claire's message was pushed to the back of her mind as Lexi remembered the other big news she had to share—exciting news about her recent history grade. Lexi started running to the monkey bars, where Claire and Eliza were already standing. Lexi was easily able to slide into their conversation about the new sixth-grade math teacher.

Their former math teacher recently moved out of town. Rumor had it he'd received a large inheritance and moved to Florida for a life on the beach. Their new teacher, Mr. Larkin, was working out pretty great, so far. Something about the way he taught and spoke with his students was different from most of Lexi's teachers. She wasn't sure what was different, but she liked him, and he seemed to enjoy teaching, which was more than she could say about several other teachers at Washington Grade School.

When the conversation ended, Lexi broke in with her news. "You guys!" she nearly shouted, "I got an A+ on my history report! I get to go with you on the class trip!"

The three girls jumped and shouted with excitement, hugging and flipping a few cartwheels before settling back down to talk details.

"Way to go, Lex, I knew you could do it!" Eliza said.

"Yeah," Claire agreed. "I've known all along you'd get to go!"

Lexi, Claire, and Eliza spent the next fifteen minutes chatting excitedly about the Six Flags trip—what they should wear, what shoes they should pack, things like that—and then practiced cartwheels until almost time for the bell to ring.

The message for Claire, which Lexi had pushed to the back of her mind, now came speeding to the front. She was about to miss her chance.

"Hey, Claire, come over here for just a sec," Lexi said as she walked a little farther away. Claire followed. Eliza glanced over with curiosity in her eyes but quickly returned to her cartwheels.

"What's up?" asked Claire.

"I just wanted to check on you and see how you're doing with your dad moving out and all."

"Oh, okay, I guess. I mostly hate that I can't do anything about the whole situation. I keep hoping I'll make them change their minds if I try hard enough, but I know that's not really going to happen." Claire looked resigned.

"I'm sorry, Claire. It must be so tough, and it's just not fair," Lexi commiserated. "Hey, I wanted to tell you something really quick before we have to go back inside. I know this might make me sound crazy, but I promise I'm not. Anyway, I was praying earlier, and I felt like God wanted me to give you a message. I feel like he's telling you 'it's not your fault' and 'trust me.'" Lexi held her breath and twisted her hands as she awaited Claire's reaction.

Seconds felt like hours as Claire stared back at her blankly. Lexi could tell she was thinking, but no words seemed able to escape her mouth.

"Claire? Are you okay? I didn't mean to upset you if I did."

Claire blinked a couple times. "No," she said. "I'm not upset. I mean, I've never heard of a kid getting a message from God before, so it *is* pretty weird."

Lexi nodded. She'd be the first to admit it was weird.

"But I'm more confused than anything, I guess. I mean, if God is really so good, why would he bother sending me a message when he could just fix my parents instead? I just don't get it. Thanks anyway, Lex. I appreciate you caring, at least."

Claire gave Lexi a quick hug just as the bell rang. Time for art. Lexi knew she needed to get her mind focused back on school. She wished the conversation had gone better, but at least Claire wasn't upset. And Lexi was glad to have obeyed.

CHAPTER 17

After an amusing attempt at painting a self-portrait during art, Lexi sat in math class, trying her best to solve a long division problem, which she couldn't imagine ever needing to do in real life. Unexpectedly, Mr. Mulvaney, the tall, grey-bearded school principal, entered the classroom. He quickly made his way to the front where Mr. Larkin stood by the whiteboard, whispered something into the teacher's ear, then exited the room. Mr. Larkin's expression turned serious.

"Lexi, may I see you at my desk please?"

Lexi stood and walked quickly to Mr. Larkin's desk. *What can this possibly be about?* She was a good student and always careful not to cause trouble at school, so surely that couldn't be the issue. But if she wasn't in trouble, what else could it be? Did Mr. Drye change his mind about her history grade and now had to tell her she couldn't go on the trip after all? Lexi had a bad feeling as she faced her teacher.

Mr. Larkin looked troubled. In a fatherly way, he put his hand on her shoulder and said, "Lexi, your mother has been in a car accident. Your father is already at the hospital, but your Aunt Hailey is here to take you and your siblings there."

Lexi froze. She suddenly felt as if everyone and everything else in the world barely existed. A car accident? What would this mean for her mom? For her family? For her? She would give up every class trip for the rest of her life if it meant her mom would be all right.

"Is she going to be okay?" she asked through tight lips.

Mr. Larkin had little comfort to offer. "She's alive, Lexi, but I don't know the extent of her injuries."

As she turned toward the doorway, he said, "I'll be praying for your mom and for your whole family."

Lexi was surprised; she'd never heard a teacher mention prayer before. "Thanks." Her voice came in a whisper as she fumbled for her backpack and exited the classroom in a daze. She found Sam and Millie waiting at the front doors. Their faces reflected the strain and worry she felt. Their mom's younger sister, Aunt Hailey, hugged Lexi when she approached. Her face was strained too.

"Let's go, kiddos."

They walked to the parking lot, still in a daze, and climbed into the back of Aunt Hailey's Honda Civic. After buckling their seatbelts, they set off for the hospital. The fifteen-minute drive across town felt like an eternity.

Lexi's mind turned to God. Mr. Larkin had said he would pray for them, but now Claire's voice rang in Lexi's head—*If God is really so good, why wouldn't he just fix my parents?* At the time, Lexi had dismissed the question, thinking that Claire just didn't understand God. But now ... now the same thoughts ran madly through her own mind.

Lexi's mom was one of the kindest, most loving people she knew. *How could God even let this happen to begin with? If he's really good, he would have stopped it from happening. What if Mom is badly hurt? What if ... what if she doesn't make it?*

Lexi's heart ached painfully at the thought, and she could barely breathe. Thoughts swirled through her brain like a tornado—not a small dust tornado this time, but a giant, monstrous, ugly tornado that swoops through and destroys entire towns.

As tears threatened to spill down her cheeks, last night's conversation with her mom popped into her head. She had told Lexi something important. *What was that verse again? Oh yeah. For God has not given us a spirit of fear ...*

The *only* thing Lexi felt in that moment was fear. If God hadn't given her this fear, then where did it come from? How could she *not* be fearful when she didn't even know what was going to happen to her own mother?

The Enemy.

Miss Kate had mentioned him before, but Lexi hadn't given him much thought. She had been taught in simple terms that God is good and the Enemy is bad. In that moment, she knew *he* was the one giving her a spirit of fear—the Enemy.

She knew if she truly wanted to believe God was good (and how she wanted it to be true), then now was the time to give him a chance to show his goodness. Her world was spinning out of control anyway, what did she have to lose?

Just as she spotted the hospital down the street, Lexi prayed a silent prayer. *Holy Spirit, if you're listening, please help. Hold on to my mom and help her be okay. Give her peace and help her not be afraid. Help my dad and the rest of us too. We're really scared. Amen.*

Her aunt pulled into the hospital parking garage, and after what seemed like forever, they finally found a parking spot at the very top of the winding garage. They took the elevators down and rushed inside. Mr. Hanson was waiting near the entrance, along with Grandma and Grandpa Young, her mom's and Aunt Hailey's parents.

"She's in surgery." Mr. Hanson's face was grave as he gathered them all into one giant hug. "At this point, no one can tell how bad of shape she's in. She was unconscious when they took her back."

CHAPTER 18

The hours in the waiting room were the longest of Lexi's life. How could time possibly move so slowly? Her dad, Grandma and Grandpa Young, and Aunt Hailey used the time to make phone calls, asking for prayer from relatives, friends, and pastors. Lexi and her siblings stared blankly at a cartoon that played on a small TV in the corner of the large, brightly lit room.

Aunt Hailey came over to give them money for a snack from the vending machine, and Lexi watched as Millie spent nearly ten minutes making her choice. Sam took his time too. Vending machines were usually a special treat, but without any thought, Lexi chose a bag of plain potato chips. They were tasteless, but she ate them anyway, to have something in her stomach. They had left school right before lunch.

As Lexi crunched her potato chips (which might as well have been little pieces of cardboard), her thoughts drifted back to church. Miss Kate's words from a couple of weeks ago rang in her mind: "The first thing to remember is that God is always good. Even when bad things happen, the fact that God is good never changes." *Even when bad things happen ...*

"The second thing is that God is always with us. This means when bad things happen, God is right by our side the whole time. He carries us through the hard times and gives us supernatural strength and peace." *God is always with us, and he carries us through the hard times ...*

"Lastly, I've learned no matter how hard I try, I will never be able to understand exactly how God works. Admitting I can't always understand God has been very comforting to me ... Then I don't feel like I constantly have to figure him out." *I don't always have to figure him out ...*

Lexi swallowed hard as she tried with all her might to believe these words were true.

"Remember how much I love you."

Lexi jumped where she sat and quickly looked around to find the voice that had spoken to her. There was no one. No one talking to her, anyway. She closed her eyes. Maybe she was hearing things.

But that voice! She suddenly recognized the voice she just heard as the same one she had heard before recess only two hours ago—the same voice that had given her encouragement to share with Claire.

Lexi almost forgot that before the Holy Spirit gave her a word for Claire, he had spoken directly to *her!* And apparently, since she'd nearly forgotten, he had just repeated himself.

"Remember how much I love you," he had said, twice now.

The Holy Spirit had spoken this into her heart before her mom's car accident even happened, almost as if trying to prepare Lexi's mind and heart for what lay ahead.

Even though Lexi didn't understand why all this was happening, even though she was mad God didn't prevent the accident in the first place, and even though she was scared to trust anything or anybody right now, Lexi discovered she could breathe a little more normally. Her chest muscles weren't as tight and achy as they were moments before.

Right then, Lexi settled it in her spirit to let God carry her and her family. She decided not to spend her energy trying to figure out God or tell him what to do, but to simply hold on to his goodness as truth and trust him.

Her head was still swimming with a jumble of thoughts. She was still scared and worried, but a peace that could only be supernatural was taking the edge off, and her mind was a bit more settled. *So this is what it feels like to let God carry you through a hard time. Still hard, for sure, but peaceful-hard, not out-of-control-hard.*

Ten minutes ago, Lexi could hardly breathe, hardly think, hardly notice the people around her. Now she decided there was nothing else to do but trust God to see her family through. Even during the never-ending wait while her mother was in surgery, she was determined to hold on to God and the hope he offered.

Lexi looked over at Sam and Millie. They were attempting to sit still but didn't seem to know what to do with themselves. "You guys want to have a tic-tac-toe tournament?" she asked, attempting to distract her siblings, as well as herself.

"Yes!" they answered at the same time.

"Okay, you guys find some paper and pens, and I'll be ready in a second." Lexi walked over to her father who had finally run out of people to call. She said a silent prayer that the Holy Spirit would bring peace and strength to her dad, then gave him a big hug.

"I love you, Daddy," she said. "Whatever is going on back there with Mom, I know God's holding on to her."

Mr. Hanson hugged her tightly, his chin pressing into her hair. "Thank you, Lex ... but it seems that *I* should be the one comforting *you* right now." As he offered an apologetic smile, fresh tears pooled in his eyes. "I love you, sweetheart."

Lexi gave his hand a squeeze and turned back toward the short, round table where Sam and Millie were waiting with paper and pens. Grandma and Grandpa Young joined the game, and after thirty minutes of Xs and Os, they awarded Grandpa the title of "Official Tic-Tac-Toe Champion." Millie even crafted a first-place ribbon for him from a spare piece of paper.

CHAPTER 19

After Grandpa Young emerged the victor of the tic-tac-toe tournament, everyone settled back down to watch TV while the never-ending wait continued. Glancing at her father, Lexi noticed he had taken the waiting room Bible off the small end table and was flipping through the pages, stopping occasionally to read a passage more thoroughly.

As Lexi sat with nothing to do, she thought back to just a few short hours ago when she learned she had earned an A+ on her Revolutionary War report and would get to go on the class trip. She couldn't remember ever being so excited in her life. Then she had given Claire the message from the Holy Spirit. That hadn't gone quite so well, but Lexi still felt good about having obeyed.

And now this. The blissful bubble of the morning had burst, and there she sat—in a hospital waiting room with nothing to do but wait to find out the fate of her own mother. The fate of their entire family, really. Strange how quickly things could change.

Just when Lexi was beginning to think the surgery would last forever, a tall, important-looking doctor dressed in crisp surgical scrubs walked into the room. Lexi's father, grandparents, and aunt were immediately at his side. His nametag read *Dr. Lee,* and he seemed aware of the family's wait and worry. Thankfully, he wasted no time getting to the point.

"Your wife is a lucky woman, sir," Dr. Lee said to Mr. Hanson.

Lexi's dad inhaled as if he hadn't taken a breath all day, and color began returning to his face. Until that moment, Lexi hadn't even realized the color was missing.

"For all intents and purposes, after the severity of the car accident, Mrs. Hanson shouldn't be alive right now. She has suffered only two fractured ribs and a ruptured spleen, along with quite a bit of bruising. The rupture was contained, so there wasn't a dangerous amount of blood lost."

The adults in the room breathed sighs of relief while Lexi gasped— that sounded terrible! *What does he mean only a ruptured spleen and some fractured ribs! What is a spleen, anyway? Surely a person can't live without their spleen! And why is the doctor acting like it's no big deal? Doesn't he know this is my mother he's talking about?*

Dr. Lee went on, "We removed all fragments of the spleen. A person can live a completely normal life without one, other than being a bit more susceptible to illnesses and infections. Her operation site and ribs will take six to eight weeks to heal all together, which means you guys ..." He paused to look at Lexi, Sam, and Millie. "... will have to be great helpers at home." He winked and turned his attention back to the adults.

Wait, is Dr. Lee really saying Mom is going to be okay? How is that possible? Lexi had overheard some of the details of the car accident after they had arrived, and everyone seemed to think that her mom even being alive was a miracle. Her father had clearly been bracing himself for a worse report.

Lexi sat in the closest chair she could find and closed her eyes. She breathed more deeply than she had since before getting called to Mr. Larkin's desk a few long hours ago. All she could think was, *Thank you, God. Thank you for saving my mom.*

Dr. Lee made sure Mr. Hanson was aware his wife would need several more hours before awaking from the anesthesia and being able to receive visitors, then he quietly exited the room.

Lexi sighed. More waiting. At least this time the wait wouldn't be quite so stressful, since they had already received the incredible news that her mom would be back to normal in a couple of months. Funny how a couple hours of waiting for the surgery to end felt like an eternity just a short time ago, but a couple months for her mom to heal sounded like no time at all.

Lexi and her family made the long hike downstairs to the hospital cafeteria for a bite to eat while they waited. Nothing looked particularly appetizing, but Lexi chose a large, homemade-looking Rice Krispies treat wrapped in cellophane. There wasn't much talking at their table as they ate their snacks. They threw away their trash while they waited on Millie, the slowest eater of the bunch, to finish her apple slices before making the long walk back upstairs, through the maze of hallways, to wait some more.

Lexi was glad to find only a few other people using the waiting room when she and her family settled back in. After an hour of playing I Spy and

Twenty Questions with Aunt Hailey and Grandma Young, and another hour watching cartoons and flipping through waiting room magazines, a nurse with a neat gray bun stepped into the doorway. Her business-like eyes scanned the room and landed on Lexi's dad.

"Are you Mr. Hanson, Linda's husband?"

"Yes, that's me. How's my wife?"

"Everything went well with the surgery. She woke up a little while ago, and we removed her ventilator. She has been resting, going in and out of sleep. You all may come see her, but only for a few minutes. She's going to be very sore and needs a lot of rest. She will have to remain in the hospital for at least the next three days so we can monitor her progress."

Lexi and the rest of the family joined her dad, who followed the nurse down the long, extra-wide, peach-colored hallway. Lexi disliked the odor that wafted through the halls. Smells of ointment and sickness filled her nose. After turning the corner and walking down an even longer hallway, they finally arrived at room 422, her mother's room. *Linda* was scrawled in red marker across a small whiteboard near the doorway.

The family gingerly crowded into the small room. Lexi had never seen her mom so helpless before. Tears immediately threatened, but she choked them back. She knew all would be okay eventually, but in this moment, Lexi felt scared. She wanted her mom to climb out of bed, wrap her robe over her pajamas, and drive home with them like everything was fine. But everything wasn't fine. At least not yet.

Suddenly, Lexi felt a warmth flow through her body, slowing her worries, making her mind begin to feel more peaceful. It took only a second for Lexi to recognize the work of the Holy Spirit. Her new friend. Her Comforter.

Lexi knew the Holy Spirit was in the room, giving them strength and peace, and she silently offered up a quick prayer of thanks. She knew her family couldn't handle this in their own strength.

Though the doctor had said so before, Lexi now had a newfound confidence that her mom *would* get better. She was a fighter and wouldn't let this get her down any longer than necessary. Then life could get back to normal.

Mrs. Hanson opened her eyes as the family gathered around her bed. She blinked a few times, as if trying to remember what was going on.

"The medication hasn't entirely worn off yet," the nurse explained. "Once the anesthesia is completely out of her system, she'll be much more alert."

Mr. Hanson bent down and kissed his wife on her forehead, carefully avoiding the bruises. Aunt Hailey held her sister's hand while Grandma and Grandpa Young stroked their daughter's hair. Lexi was afraid to touch her mom—she didn't want to add to the pain. Lexi's eyes met her dad's, and he gave her a slight nod. Ever so lightly, she rubbed her mother's shoulder and spoke in a voice barely above a whisper, "Hi, Mom."

Lexi gazed into her mother's eyes and was startled to see how content she looked, lying helpless in a hospital bed. Her eyes shone with peace, not fear or pain as Lexi had feared.

Mrs. Hanson tried to speak, but her throat was too dry to form a sound. Mr. Hanson located a large thermos with a straw on a small table nearby and gave her a sip of water. She tried again.

"I wasn't alone," she said, somewhat dazedly. Her voice was gravelly. "... didn't know what was happening ... heard a voice say to keep holding on, keep your eyes on me. ... God was carrying me ... I was scared, then it was so peaceful." Her eyes closed again as she drifted off.

The nurse walked forward and put her hand on Mr. Hanson's shoulder. "Mrs. Hanson needs her rest now. We'll call for you again when she wakes up."

The family exited the small room and returned to the all-too-familiar waiting room. Lexi looked over at Sam and Millie. They still looked a little scared but, overall, seemed to be doing okay. This was a lot for everybody to take in.

Her mom's words played over and over in Lexi's mind as they walked down the long, peach hallway. *I wasn't alone ... heard a voice say to keep holding on ... God was carrying me ... so peaceful."*

Unable to hold back tears any longer, Lexi wept. She didn't care that several strangers in the hall turned to look as she passed—she hardly noticed. She grabbed a tissue from the nurse's station and continued down the hall, crying tears of sadness for her family and tears of relief that her mom was going to be okay. Mostly, she cried tears of joy that the Holy Spirit had so dramatically answered her prayers to hold on to her mother in the middle of all the chaos and confusion.

POWER UP

After experiencing the Holy Spirit in such a real way, Lexi couldn't imagine ever doubting his existence again.

CHAPTER 20

Lexi dried her tears as they returned to the waiting room, then let her body drop onto an armchair, exhausted. Again, she prayed for strength and peace. She knew now for sure—she couldn't do this without the Holy Spirit's help.

Mr. Hanson walked over to where they had just settled back in. "Kids, your mother is going to be here at the hospital until at least Thursday. I spoke with my boss, and the company is allowing me to take this week off, so I can stay here with her. Aunt Hailey will take you guys home tonight and stay with you at the house. I'll be sleeping in your mother's room," he said, eyeing the small, firm recliner in the corner, identical to the one in his wife's hospital room.

"I will let you miss school tomorrow so you can be here with your mom, but Aunt Hailey and Grandma will take turns making sure you get to and from school every other day this week. Sound okay?"

Sam and Millie nodded. Lexi stood and slipped her arm around Aunt Hailey. "Yep, sounds like a plan. We'll be fine, Dad. I'm sorry you have to sleep in a chair, though." She gave him a weak, but reassuring smile.

"Don't go worrying about me; I'll be just fine." He mustered a smile. "Come on. Let's go back downstairs for some supper before you head home. The nurse will call me if your mom wakes up."

After a meal of cafeteria cheeseburgers and fries that left Lexi and her siblings longing for McDonald's, they hugged their dad goodnight and asked him to pass their love on to their mom when she woke up.

After big hugs from Grandma and Grandpa Young, they made the long walk with Aunt Hailey to her car. Though the spring evening was warm, Lexi shivered in the humid night air.

Fifteen minutes later, Aunt Hailey pulled her Civic up to the Hansons' white, two-story house. Lexi had always loved their house, which was in a subdivision on the outskirts of town. The subdivision was older, and all the lots were at least an acre. They had a large, welcoming front porch, lots of big maple and oak trees, and plenty of space to run and play. Lexi had lived there her whole life and hoped to stay until she got married someday. She remembered the picture the Holy Spirit had recently given her of her loving, cozy home. Now she understood.

Aunt Hailey unlocked the front door, and they trudged in, ready to get some rest in the comfort of their own rooms. Lexi had always thought their house was the coziest house she knew, but this was the first time she could remember walking in without her mother near. If her mom wasn't coming and going with Lexi and her siblings, she was usually busy doing something in the kitchen, weeding the flowers around the porch, or sitting in the dining room window seat with a book and a steaming mug of black coffee (or occasionally tea) in hand.

Lexi felt a lump in her throat as she determinedly reminded herself that her mother was going to be fine. She was shocked to realize how much the comfort of their home depended on her mom's presence.

Lexi gave her head a shake—her brain felt fuzzy. She needed to brush her teeth and get to bed. The day had been exhausting, and she could barely think straight.

Years ago, her mom had told her that things usually seemed brighter in the morning, and Lexi found, for some reason, the saying was true. She whispered another quick prayer of thanks and protection for her mom before her head hit the pillow.

CHAPTER 21

When Lexi's eyes opened the next morning, she had to remind herself what was going on. Her mom had been in a car accident, but was going to be fine. Eventually. No school today. Aunt Hailey was there with them. Lexi stretched, then climbed reluctantly from under her warm covers. She slowly got dressed, then washed her face with cold water, trying to wake herself up. As soon as she was ready, she headed downstairs like any other day.

Lexi was used to the sight of her mom making breakfast, and quickly blinked back tears at the memory. This time, she found Aunt Hailey downstairs, sitting in the dining room window seat with a cup of coffee in hand and a Bible spread open on her lap. At first glance, Aunt Hailey looked so much like her mother that Lexi had to look again.

Aunt Hailey stood to give Lexi a hug and offer her a bowl of cereal. "How did you sleep, honey? Are you hungry?"

"I slept pretty well. Yesterday must have worn me out. Did you sleep okay?" Lexi grabbed a bowl and spoon that Aunt Hailey had set out, and a box of strawberry shredded wheat from the cereal cabinet.

"Not too bad. You guys have a super comfy couch." Aunt Hailey smiled wearily as she carried her stoneware mug to the coffee pot to pour a second cup.

"After your brother and sister are up and everyone has eaten breakfast, we'll go back over to the hospital. I spoke with your dad earlier this morning, and he said your mom had a decent night and has a little more energy today, which are good signs!"

Lexi was glad they would be going back soon. She wanted to spend as much time as possible with her mom before going back to school tomorrow.

Aunt Hailey and Lexi turned to see Sam and Millie racing down the stairs. Sam skipped the last four steps entirely with a huge leap, landing with a hard thud.

"Cereal—yay!" Sam shouted enthusiastically. Aunt Hailey reached out to steal a quick hug, and he paused just long enough to reciprocate. Millie walked over to Aunt Hailey and silently reached her arms up to be held. Aunt Hailey gladly obliged, sharing some cuddles before placing Millie in her seat for breakfast.

As soon as the breakfast dishes were cleared, they piled into the car. The drive to the hospital was somber, but thankfully, not as stressful as yesterday.

Lexi was relieved to find her mother acting more herself when they arrived. Though still very sore and tired, she was more alert and visibly glad to see them.

The day passed slowly as her mother rotated between napping and chatting with visitors. By then, many family friends and pastors had heard about the accident and dropped in to visit, pray, and offer their support to the family.

Lexi and her family spent much of their time in the waiting room, visiting with Mrs. Hanson in room 422 as often as they were allowed by hospital staff, and as long as no other visitors were waiting for a turn.

Lexi badly wanted to share her exciting news about getting an A+ on her history report, but she knew now wasn't the right time or place. For the first time, the thought crossed her mind that she might not even get to go on the class trip. What if she were needed at home?

Sam and Millie were still young, but Lexi was old enough to help with her siblings and do some cooking and cleaning. She groaned inwardly at the thought of staying home, then scolded herself. *If I'm needed at home, I'm needed at home, and that's that.* She would have to find out one way or another. Permission slips were due next week.

Lexi and her siblings kissed their mom goodbye late that afternoon, and Grandma and Grandpa Young, who had also been at the hospital all day, took them home to prepare for school the next day. Lexi was thankful her mom was improving, so being away from her for the night wasn't as nerve-wracking.

After settling back in at home, Grandma checked the voicemail on the home phone.

"Lexi!" she called up the stairs, "there's a message for you from your friend Eliza!"

Lexi rushed down the stairs to listen to the message: "Hi, Lexi. It's Eliza. I just wanted to call and tell you how sorry I am about your mom. I hope you're doing okay. Let me know if you need anything. Bye!"

Lexi smiled at Eliza's thoughtfulness.

As she started back toward her room, the phone rang. Grandma answered and again held the phone out toward Lexi, who was halfway up the stairs. "One of your friends," Grandma whispered, her hand covering the mouthpiece.

Lexi took the phone. "Hello?"

"Hey, Lexi! It's Claire. Are you okay? I heard about your mom."

"Hey, Claire. I'm doing okay, I guess. It's all been pretty scary, but she's going to get better. Thanks for checking. How are you?"

"I'm fine. I have your school make-up assignments from the last couple days, and I wondered if my mom could bring me by to drop them off. I have Sam's and Millie's too."

"Oh, thanks, that would be super helpful!"

"Okay! See you in a few minutes. Bye!" Claire hung up.

Lexi had all but forgotten about schoolwork during the craziness of the last couple days. She appreciated Claire going to the trouble of bringing their assignments over.

Ten minutes later, there was a knock at the front door. Lexi opened the door to find Claire standing on the front porch with a tote bag full of school work. On the front of the tote bag was a large picture of a green leaf with the words *Keep it Simple* scrolled underneath. Lexi chuckled to herself. *If only.*

She took the bag from her friend. "Thank you so much for bringing this over, Claire. It was so nice of you to get Sam and Millie's homework too. Do you want to come inside?"

"Thanks, but I can't. Mom's waiting in the car." Claire gestured toward the curb where her mother was parked. Lexi peered through the darkness and saw Claire's mom wave from her car. Lexi waved back.

"I know your mom is the most important thing right now, Lex, but … will you still be able to go to Six Flags?" Claire asked cautiously, as if reading Lexi's mind.

"Good question. I need to talk to my dad and find out. I just don't want to bother him yet."

"I understand. I really hope it works out. It wouldn't be the same without you."

"Thanks. And thanks again for bringing this. I really appreciate it. Well, sort of …" Lexi smiled as she peeked through the bag and saw her dreaded history homework. At least she had earned her B in the class for the trip and there wasn't as much pressure for the last few weeks of the school year.

Claire laughed. "No problem. You've been so encouraging to me since finding out about my dad, I just wanted to do something nice back." She pointed at Lexi as if she'd just remembered something. "And hey, I was thinking about your invitation to go to church with you, and thought maybe I'd go after all. Do you think you'll still go this weekend?"

Lexi hesitated. "I don't really know; I *think* my dad will probably still take us and leave Aunt Hailey or my grandparents here with my mom. She should be back home by then. How about we plan on it, but I'll let you know if we don't end up going."

"Sounds good," Claire agreed. "Okay, then, I'll see you in school and hopefully at church too. Have a good night!"

Claire turned and walked down the steps. Lexi paused, then cried out, "Wait!"

Claire stopped mid-stride and turned.

"What made you change your mind?" Lexi asked.

Claire thought for a second before replying. "I guess I just want to see what's going on with all this Holy Spirit stuff. You seem pretty convinced, so I thought I'd check it out for myself."

She grinned at Lexi, then turned and headed back to the car. Lexi smiled to herself as she lugged the heavy homework bag into the house to distribute to her siblings. She thought of Claire's new curiosity about church, and wondered what the Holy Spirit was up to.

Lexi wasn't quite as exhausted as she'd been the night before, so after climbing in bed and grabbing her purple pillow to hug, she lay awake, thinking. The events of the day flashed through her mind in pieces. She was thankful her mom was improving, but she knew the road would still be long. Her mom's ribs wouldn't be healed for over a month, which meant they would definitely need extra help around the house. Lexi really hoped her dad wouldn't ask her to stay home and miss Six Flags.

Offer.

Offer? Where did that come from? Offer what? Lexi's mind was so full her thoughts were jumping around all over the place. She tried to think of the following school day. Of seeing her friends again.

Offer.

What was going on? Why was she imagining voices in her head? Lexi tried to clear her mind. To focus on not thinking of anything, even though she knew that never worked.

Offer.

Shoot. There it was again.

And she knew.

From the first time she heard the voice, she knew in her heart the Holy Spirit was speaking. He was telling her to offer to stay home from Six Flags.

But what if she didn't *want* to offer? What if she pretended she never heard the instruction at all?

Tears filled her eyes. She knew she couldn't do that. She remembered Miss Kate telling them God's way was always best, even when they didn't understand. This must be one of those times.

Lexi squeezed her pillow with all her might. She had worked so hard for so many weeks, dreaming of going to Six Flags with her friends. And now the dream had been taken away. Just like that. She didn't understand why the Holy Spirit would ask her to give this up.

It wasn't fair.

She knew she'd never be able to figure God out this time, so she fought back her frustration and tried with all her might, like she had done in the hospital, to trust that God was still good.

Her grip on the pillow loosened but her jaw clenched as she resolved to speak with her dad the next day and make the offer to stay home. Tears began to flow freely, splotching her comforter. Tears for her mom. For the trip. Finally, when Lexi was too exhausted to cry another tear, her eyes closed, now beyond her control, and she escaped into the respite of sleep.

93

CHAPTER 22

Lexi's classmates milled around at school the next morning, checking on her and inquiring about her mom. Lexi appreciated the attention. It felt good to know so many people cared, but she did hope her eyes weren't noticeably puffy from all the crying she'd done the night before.

All their questions had the same answers:

"My mom is getting better, but it will take a couple months before she's back to normal."

"It's hard, but I'm doing okay."

"God is really taking care of us."

Most of her classmates smiled and nodded in understanding, but she did notice a few kids with strange expressions on their faces at her mention of God.

At recess, Lexi met up with her friends, answering all their questions and sharing her appreciation for their concern. She was thankful Claire and Eliza were becoming her true friends—not just see-you-at-recess friends, but friends who really cared about one another.

The conversation about her mom finally came to an end, and Lexi turned to Claire. "How have you been doing with your dad moving out and everything?"

"I think I'm okay," Claire replied. "He got an apartment across town, so I'll still get to see him a lot. He's moving out this Saturday."

Eliza wore a sympathetic expression but didn't seem to know what to say.

"I'm sorry." Lexi scrunched her eyebrows together. Even though she was frustrated the Holy Spirit wanted her to offer to stay home from the trip, she still wanted to tell Claire about the comfort he could bring. "One thing I'm learning from my mom's accident is that hard situations are a whole lot easier to handle when you let the Holy Spirit help you. I know it sounds weird, but seriously, he gave me *so* much peace while I was at the hospital and worried about my mom. The difference was kind of incredible."

Claire just smiled. "Are we on for church this Sunday?"

"Yep, my dad said he would pick you up on the way and drop you off after lunch."

Eliza looked at them, confused, and Lexi quickly realized Eliza had been left out of the whole church conversation. "You're invited to come too, if you want! It would be awesome if you could."

Eliza looked curious but politely declined. "Thanks anyway, but I already have plans for Sunday morning … plans to sleep as late as possible!" She laughed. "Maybe a different time though."

Oh well. Maybe she'll think about it at least. Lexi smiled at her friend.

After art class came math, and as students were finding their seats, Mr. Larkin gestured for Lexi to come up to his desk.

"Yes, Mr. Larkin?"

"I just wanted to check and see how you and your family are doing. How is your mother?"

"We're doing okay, thanks. Things are kind of hard, but my mom is going to be okay eventually."

"I'm so glad. I've kept your family in prayer since we found out about the accident."

"Thanks, Mr. Larkin." Lexi smiled with appreciation before returning to her desk. Now she knew, for sure, the difference between him and the other teachers. She knew there were rules regarding teachers discussing God in school, but she was comforted to know at least one teacher at Washington Grade School believed in God and was bold enough to say so.

After school, Aunt Hailey took Lexi, Sam, and Millie back to the hospital for a visit. Lexi hadn't seen much of her dad that week, so when she found him in the waiting room, she immediately ran to give him a giant hug.

"How's Mom?" she asked, once his strong arms released her.

"She's had a pretty good day. She just fell asleep, but will probably be up in about an hour, so you guys should get to spend some time with her before you have to head home. The nurse is supposed to text me when she wakes up."

While Sam, Millie, and Aunt Hailey found seats by a low table, which held coloring books and a box of broken crayons, Lexi pulled her dad aside. She was afraid if she didn't talk to him right then and make the offer, she might talk herself out of it. Once more, she silently asked the Holy Spirit if he was sure, hoping maybe he had changed his mind.

Offer.

Lexi grimaced. No luck.

She spoke quickly, so she wouldn't chicken out. "Dad, I know we haven't had a chance to talk lately, but I wanted to let you know I got an A+ on my history report, which earned me a B+ in the class overall." She paused to steady her voice. "I was planning to go on our class trip in a couple weeks, but I know you'll need extra help at home while Mom is getting better, so ..."

Lexi almost couldn't speak the words aloud. She wished she could go color with her brother and sister and forget she ever brought the trip up. But she knew what she had to do. She felt a flood of encouragement and strength.

"I want to offer to stay home and help," she finished. There. She'd done it. Good-bye trip, hello housework. Lexi knew she had done the right thing, and for that reason she felt peaceful, if not particularly happy.

Her dad's eyes widened. "Lex, I don't know what to say. First of all, I'm so proud of you for working so hard to get your history grade up. I know that wasn't easy. And second ..." His voice trailed off and his eyes glistened. "You've just grown up so much." He cleared his throat and rested his hands on her shoulders. "I know how much you've been looking forward to Six Flags, and the fact that you're offering to stay home tells me what a mature young lady you've become. I'm sure it was a difficult offer for you to make."

Lexi nodded and took a deep breath, fighting back tears that threatened to spill down her face at any moment, an event that was becoming more and more common these days.

Her dad went on, "Lexi, I want you to go to Six Flags with your friends. I know Mom will feel the same. I already talked to work about taking extra time off anyway, and with your grandparents and aunt around, we'll manage just fine. You earned this trip. You should go."

He smiled, pulled her into his arms, and spoke softly. "I'm so proud of you, Lex. Thank you for the selfless offer."

Lexi couldn't wrap her brain around what just happened. She had settled it in her mind last night that she would miss the trip. Hadn't the Holy Spirit told her to stay home? Did she really get to go on the trip after all? She hugged her dad back, tightly. He rumpled her hair, then walked over to talk to Aunt Hailey. In a daze, Lexi lowered herself into an empty chair.

Well done.

She recognized the voice more easily this time.

After reflecting for a minute, Lexi realized something startling. The Holy Spirit never *had* told her she wouldn't be able to go—he had simply told her to offer. And now he was telling her *well done*. She hadn't exactly wanted to obey, but she had anyway.

Miss Kate's words immediately came to mind. "The important part is that you are obedient. Sometimes that's God's whole plan all along. He'll use these opportunities to help us grow into braver, more powerful children of God."

If spirituality was really like a muscle, as Miss Kate had said, Lexi sure was getting a workout lately—and becoming stronger. She felt filled with supernatural peace after obeying God and putting her family first.

And she would still get to go on the trip! She honestly couldn't believe it was true. School couldn't come fast enough—she could hardly wait until the next day to tell Claire and Eliza all that had happened. She wanted to squeal with joy right then and there, but forced herself to contain it, being in a hospital and all. Lexi took a deep breath to steady herself. What a rollercoaster of a day.

CHAPTER 23

Thursday morning, Lexi immediately popped out of bed and ran downstairs. Aunt Hailey had spent the night with them so her grandparents could be at the hospital.

"Aunt Hailey!" she cried. "Mom gets to come home today!"

Sam and Millie were already at the table, about to dig into their scrambled eggs and toast, but they jumped up when Lexi came down the stairs. Millie led them in a celebratory dance around the table as they chanted in sing-song voices, "Mom's coming home today! Mom's coming home today!" The heavy atmosphere had finally lifted, and an energy, missing all week, filled them all.

Aunt Hailey laughed. "You guys aren't excited or anything, right?" Her eyes twinkled.

Lexi, Sam, and Millie finally stopped their dance and sat down for breakfast. This had been the longest week of their lives, with their mom in the hospital and their dad staying with her. Lexi was thankful for her grandparents' and Aunt Hailey's willingness to stay with them this week. They each reminded Lexi of her mom in many ways, which was comforting.

"What time is she coming home?" Sam asked. He fidgeted in his seat so much, his chair almost toppled over.

"Well," Aunt Hailey replied, "by the time they do final check-ups and sign all the paperwork to release her, it will probably be late afternoon. You guys should be able to go to school and get back before they come home."

Lexi was disappointed to have such a long school day ahead, but there was nothing she could do. She finished her breakfast and got dressed. Soon she was sitting on the bus on her way to another mundane day of school. Her thoughts rotated between her mom and Six Flags. She still hardly dared to believe she could go.

After what seemed an endless school day, the yellow bus finally pulled to a stop in front of the Hansons' house. Lexi, Sam, and Millie ran inside, threw their backpacks in the closet, and found Aunt Hailey, looking over some papers at the kitchen counter.

"Hi, kids! Your mom and dad will be home in about twenty minutes!" Aunt Hailey passed out hugs. "And just a reminder—your mom is still extremely sore from all she's been through. She won't be able to get around the house by herself yet, which means your dad will be spending a lot of time helping her." They had already prepared themselves. They were just glad she was coming home.

Millie had the idea to throw together a quick surprise party, so the next twenty minutes were a flurry of activity. Lexi blew up balloons (being the only one besides Aunt Hailey who could tie them), Millie decorated the living room by draping streamers everywhere she could reach, and Sam taped together four pieces of white paper to make a big sign that read: *WELCUM HOM MOMMY*. He quickly taped it to the living room wall just before the front door swung open.

In walked Grandma, Grandpa, and finally their dad, carefully pushing their mother in a wheelchair.

A wheelchair? Lexi hadn't considered the need for a wheelchair, but she realized the assistance made sense for now. She would just have to get used to it.

All three kids crowded around and gently kissed their mom's cheeks. She was still too sore for hugs, but that didn't stop her from asking them to lean in so she could kiss them back. Lexi was thankful she was alert and seemed herself again.

As Mr. Hanson pushed his wife into the living room, Lexi watched her mother's eyes become teary as she took in the sign and the decorations. Her mom always did cry easily—while reading a good book, watching a sad commercial, or just about any other reason under the sun. Lexi could see the emotion in her mother's tears this time, and she understood.

"Thank you, kids. You have no idea how good it feels to be home."

"Well, I do," Mr. Hanson added, "and it feels wonderful!" He reached out to hug his children, one by one. "We both missed you kids very much."

CHAPTER 24

Lexi volunteered to make breakfast Sunday morning before church. Since her mom had come home Thursday, they'd all spent a few days trying to find a new family rhythm. Lexi was glad to help. She was also glad her dad had gotten some extra time off work.

The only things Lexi knew how to make besides cereal were fried eggs and toast. Standing at the stove while Sam and Millie ran around the house, playing chase or tag or whatever it was they were doing, she tried not to be jealous. After all, she had offered to make breakfast, and helping out did feel good. Lexi did her best to ignore the shouts and laughter coming from the living room.

Sliding the spatula under an almost-done egg, Lexi discovered the egg had nearly glued itself to the bottom of the pan. She sighed and made a mental note to grease the skillet next time. Then her thoughts turned to Claire. Her dad had moved out yesterday—she wondered how Claire was dealing with everything. Staring into the sizzling pan of fried eggs in front of her, Lexi whispered, "Holy Spirit, please give Claire the same peace you gave me in the hospital. Give her extra strength to deal with this and help her know how much you love her. Amen."

After thirty minutes of fumbling with egg shells, butter knives, and spatulas, Lexi carried a plate to the living room, where her mom was comfortably situated. The plate held one egg and a piece of toast with extra butter, just the way her mom preferred. Lexi noticed, for some reason, the butter wasn't melting like when her mom made toast. Next time, she would try making the toast last instead of first.

The rest of the family gathered at the dining room table where the remaining eggs and toast were waiting. They polished off breakfast in no time, and Lexi's dad thanked her for cooking.

"My little girl is growing up," he said, wistfully. "I remember when you wanted to get up early on Sundays to help me make breakfast before church. And now you've become a great cook all on your own. Thanks again for breakfast, sweetie." He smiled gratefully as he finished off his cold toast.

Since Mrs. Hanson couldn't move from place to place easily, she spent most of her days in the living room. For a family who didn't watch much TV, the television had been getting quite a workout. Lexi's mom watched mostly cooking shows and reruns of her favorite old sitcoms. *I Love Lucy* was one of Lexi's favorites; she always joined her mom on the couch as soon as she heard the opening theme song. Lexi secretly pictured Millie growing up to be like Lucy. The thought made her laugh.

Lexi's grandparents and Aunt Hailey soon arrived to spend the morning with Linda while everyone else went to church. The kids gave their mom a gentle hug goodbye (her bruising and stitches were still tender) and piled into the car.

"Time to go pick up Claire!" Lexi announced. Nerves fluttered in her stomach at the thought of what the morning would hold and how Claire would respond, but excitement soon overtook the nerves. Lexi smiled. Her mom was home, her friend wanted to come to church with her, and there was a class trip to look forward to. Life was good.

Ten minutes later they were at Claire's house, and she was climbing into the back of their SUV. Once they were alone in the backseat, Lexi whispered, "Claire, how are you doing after your dad left yesterday? Honestly."

Claire looked tired, as if she'd already had an extra-long weekend. "I'm hanging in there," she said, mustering a smile. "Going to church with you guys is a good distraction."

"Well," Lexi said, "I'm really glad you changed your mind and decided to come. I know yesterday had to be tough, but hopefully you can enjoy this morning."

Claire looked puzzled when they arrived and Mr. Hanson parked the car on the far side of the lot. Lexi leaned over and whispered, "He does this every week. It's his way of helping people who can't get around as easily." She shrugged. Claire silently smiled back.

As they passed through the building, Lexi noticed Claire's surprise as stranger after stranger warmly welcomed her.

When they entered the classroom, Miss Kate made a bee-line toward them. As usual, her demeanor was kind and welcoming, though this morning Lexi detected something else in her eyes. Concern, maybe.

"Good morning, Lexi, Sam, Millie. I'm very sorry to hear about your mom, but I'm so grateful she's going to be okay." Lexi and Sam thanked Miss Kate. Millie smiled shyly.

"And who do we have here?" Miss Kate asked, offering her hand to Claire.

"This is my friend, Claire," replied Lexi. "She's visiting today."

"Wonderful! My name is Miss Kate, and I'll be your teacher this morning. I'm so glad you decided to join us." Claire shook Miss Kate's hand, and Lexi could see Claire's shoulders relax at Miss Kate's kindness. "Feel free to look around and find a game or activity to do while we wait for everyone else to arrive." Miss Kate gestured toward the play shelves before turning to greet some students who had just arrived.

"She seems nice," Claire whispered as they walked across the room to search for something to occupy the next ten minutes.

"She is," Lexi whispered back. They found a word search puzzle book and two pencils and got to work. "Very."

Soon the rest of the students had arrived. "Everyone please find a seat, and we'll begin!" Miss Kate flickered the lights on and off to get everyone's attention.

The girls quickly found two seats together in the large circle of chairs. Lexi reached over and gave Claire's hand a reassuring squeeze.

CHAPTER 25

"Good morning!" Miss Kate welcomed the class. "Thank you for joining us today. I can't wait to hear the stories you have to share from this past week. Let's jump right in. Remember, last week I asked you to find a time to *ask* the Holy Spirit if he had anything to say to you, *listen*, and then *obey* whatever he may have asked of you. Does anyone want to volunteer to share your experience first?"

The students looked around at one another, clearly hoping not to go first. Finally, an eight-year-old boy named Isaac raised his hand.

Miss Kate smiled and nodded for him to begin.

"I was waiting for my mom to pick me up after baseball practice a few days ago, and I had nothing to do so I decided to try out the homework," he said. "I asked the Holy Spirit if he wanted to say anything, and after a minute, I felt like he said, 'Say hi to your neighbor.'

"I thought that was weird. We have this neighbor named Jack. He's kind of old and lives alone, and he's always out sitting on his porch with his dog when I get home. I usually just walk into my house without saying anything because I don't really know him." Isaac shrugged.

"That day, when I got home, I stopped for a minute to wave and say hi. I asked how he was, and he looked surprised at first, but then sort of smiled. He said he was fine, but his dog had just died. My mom overheard and invited him for supper, and he came. I found out he's a pretty nice guy, and I think it really cheered him up!" Isaac said. "It's kind of amazing how all that happened just because I said hi to my neighbor."

Beaming, Miss Kate praised Isaac for his obedience. "Obeying is not always easy. Sometimes we feel uncomfortable, but then things like this happen, and it's all worthwhile!"

Isaac nodded in agreement.

"Who wants to go next?" Miss Kate asked.

A ten-year-old girl named Hope hesitantly raised her hand. Miss Kate nodded for her to begin.

"I was praying for my friend last week, and I asked the Holy Spirit if he wanted me to tell her anything. A picture of a softball came into my mind, so I went and told her about it. She said she didn't even like softball, and she didn't know what I was talking about. It was pretty embarrassing," Hope admitted, dejected.

Empathy shone through Miss Kate's gaze. "I'm sorry it didn't work out better, Hope. But you know what? You asked, listened, and obeyed, and even if the picture seemed to miss the mark with your friend, the important thing is your obedience to God. Remember, that's the most important part!"

Hope mustered a smile. Lexi had to smile too. She felt sorry for Hope, but understood firsthand, now, that obedience truly was the most important part—more important than hearing words or getting pictures for others, more important than being right, and more important than feeling comfortable.

Miss Kate went on. "And be encouraged, because once in a while, after you've shared something you thought was from the Holy Spirit, but the person doesn't understand what you mean, he or she might remember what you said at a later time, and things will suddenly make sense.

"In other words, just because the softball image didn't mean anything to her when you shared the vision, it may someday. And even if not, you still did your part. Well done, Hope!"

Lexi glanced at Claire. She looked incredulous as she took everything in. Lexi wasn't sure if she was absorbing the conversation and learning about the Holy Spirit or thinking everyone there had lost their minds. She figured there was about a fifty-fifty chance, either way.

Lexi slowly raised her hand to go next. She still didn't like speaking in front of other people, but lately it had been getting easier. "This was a pretty crazy week for my family. My mom was in a car accident on Monday." The students who hadn't already heard the news gasped.

"She's going to be okay in a few months," Lexi went on, "but we were really scared when we didn't know how hurt she was yet. We were all in the waiting room, and I was starting to get really mad at God for letting the accident happen in the first place. I felt like my mind was a little out of control, and I was really upset, but then somehow this peace came over me. I remembered that God is good and the Enemy is the bad one, so all my anger should be directed at the Enemy, not God.

"The rest of the day, whenever I started getting upset or anxious, I would pray in my head, and the Holy Spirit would give me peace. It was amazing. I know my own mind wasn't making me feel peaceful because I was a mess before," Lexi admitted with a short laugh.

"We still have a long way to go because my mom can't do much right now, and she won't be back to normal for a while. But at least now I'm trusting that things will be okay … with God's help."

Lexi realized that the rest of the classroom was quiet, and when she glanced at Claire, she saw tears in her eyes. She looked at Jacob across the room. He had been listening to all the stories silently, with no discernable expression.

"Thank you so much for sharing, Lexi," said Miss Kate. "Hearing stories of the Holy Spirit taking control and bringing peace to scary situations like yours is inspiring." She squeezed Lexi's shoulder as she walked behind her, then turned to face the rest of the class. "Anyone else have a homework story to share?"

The room was quiet, so Miss Kate sat on her stool to begin the lesson when Jacob slowly raised his hand. Miss Kate looked surprised but pleased as she called on him.

"I just want to say," Jacob began, "that I sorta thought this Holy Spirit stuff was a joke before. I mean, I believe God is real and all, and I gave the Holy Spirit a try once, but it didn't work, and I got really mad. I *have* to come to church because my grandma won't let me play video games all week unless I do." He paused to give Miss Kate an apologetic half-smile. She smiled back, clearly not offended.

Jacob ran his hands through his hair and sighed. "But listening to all these stories … I don't know. I'm starting to see things a little differently, I guess. If there really is an Enemy, then he doesn't want us to think God is real, right?"

Miss Kate nodded.

"So, I guess—if there really is a Good Guy and a Bad Guy out there, I want to be on the Good Guy's team. I've known most of you a long time, so I can't exactly just call you liars and say none of your stories about the Holy Spirit are true." Jacob shifted uncomfortably in his seat.

"All I'm saying is, maybe I'll give the Holy Spirit another try. I don't really have anything to lose, and I really don't like the idea of letting the Enemy win. That's all I have to say … I didn't do the homework."

Lexi could tell Miss Kate was fighting back tears.

"Jacob, it takes a lot of courage to say what you just said. I'm so glad you've decided to give the Holy Spirit another try. Sometimes people think life becomes easy when you decide to follow God, and I'm here to tell you that's just not true." She turned to face the rest of the class.

"We still go through hard and unfair things like everyone else, and sometimes God *does* step in and change our circumstances. But even when he doesn't change things, God promises to *always* be with us and give us the strength and peace to keep going in the middle of it all—through his Holy Spirit. And that's what makes all the difference."

Lexi smiled at Jacob across the room. Claire remained silent, leaving Lexi to wonder what sort of thoughts were running through her mind.

"We'll finish up class a little early today, and you can have some free time until your parents pick you up," said Miss Kate. "This was the last week of our Holy Spirit study, but I do hope you'll continue studying him on your own. There's always more to learn."

Lexi could see that was true. Even her parents were still learning.

Miss Kate continued. "You won't be getting specific homework this week, but I do want to challenge you to make up your own homework, or goals, for this week. Keep getting to know the Holy Spirit. Explore how he can use you to encourage others, and don't forget to stop and listen. He wants to encourage each of us personally, if we will quiet ourselves and listen."

She stood and looked at each child in turn, her eyes shining.

"Also remember—this is a lifelong process. I don't have it all figured out yet, and I'm sure I never will. I can only wake up each morning and do my best to follow what God has in store for me that day. And that's all God is asking of you."

Miss Kate turned her face away from the students, picked up her giant travel mug, and took a long drink. Lexi wondered if she was holding back tears. If she was anything like Lexi's mom, it didn't take much to make her cry.

Miss Kate turned back around and cleared her throat. Her eyes looked a little red. "Thank you for going on this Holy Spirit adventure with me these past few weeks. Hopefully the journey has been as great for you as it has been for me." She finished with a smile.

"Before our snack, I'd like to say a quick prayer. Ready?" she asked. Eyes closed around the room, and Miss Kate bowed her head.

"Dear God, thank you so much for each child listening right now. Thank you for loving them and giving your Holy Spirit to them so they can live powerful new lives here on earth. I pray each child here would know you're real. Help them know you're always good, even when we don't understand what's going on. Thank you that every day is an adventure when we're following you. In Jesus's name. Amen."

When Lexi opened her eyes, she saw the other students jump up and rush to the snack table for cookies and juice. Miss Kate had brought a special snack to celebrate their last day of the Holy Spirit study. The cookies from her bakery were beautifully decorated with bright icing swirls and sprinkles.

Lexi glanced at Claire as they made their way to the snack table. She couldn't exactly identify what emotion she saw on her face, but she was beginning to think it was a look of acceptance.

CHAPTER 26

Claire was invited to stay for lunch, so while Lexi, Claire, Sam, and Millie buckled their seatbelts, Mr. Hanson took everyone's Cracker Barrel orders and called ahead to place the order. Lexi couldn't wait to get home and find out what Claire thought of church. They couldn't talk seriously about anything while they were in the car with Sam and Millie right beside them being loud and silly.

When they arrived at Cracker Barrel, Mr. Hanson ran inside to pick up their large to-go order so they could eat with the rest of the family at home. The smell of delicious food teased their hungry stomachs all the way home.

Mr. Hanson pulled the SUV into the garage, then Lexi and Claire carried the multiple bags of food inside and set them on the counter. The grown-ups weren't quite ready to sit down for lunch, so Lexi and Claire rushed up to Lexi's room and shut the door, plopping down onto the neat blue comforter. (Lexi had actually been making her bed lately.) When Lexi looked down at her blanket, she saw faint outlines of small circles here and there. Tear stains. *What a week!*

"Well," Lexi began, "what did you think of church?"

Claire sighed, then smiled. "Church was interesting, that's for sure. I've never been to one like that before. It's kind of a lot to take in. I guess I'm still trying to figure everything out."

Lexi nodded in understanding.

Claire continued, "Like, last week when you said the Holy Spirit had a message for me, you said he wanted to tell me to trust him and it wasn't my fault. I know I said I didn't know what you were talking about, but I couldn't stop thinking about those words the rest of the week. Now I wonder if the Holy Spirit is the one who keeps bringing them back up in my mind. I mean, I've been to church plenty of times, but I never knew it could become so *real.* I guess I don't know what to do next."

"Well, you could try believing what he says and see what happens," Lexi suggested.

Claire chuckled. "You make it sound so simple."

"It doesn't have to be complicated. I think God really wants you to understand how much he loves you and to know that your dad's leaving isn't your fault. Do you believe that?"

Claire's face turned serious again and her eyes teared up. "Sort of," she whispered, focusing on the thin silver bracelet dangling from her wrist. Lost in thought, she twirled the bangle around and around.

"It's true," Lexi said. "God loves you so much. What your dad did has nothing to do with you. He has his own problems to work through."

Claire straightened and looked Lexi in the eyes. "I want to believe that. I would love to truly believe you and have everything be as simple as you make it sound." She paused. "But how do I make myself?"

"You can't make yourself," Lexi said. "You need to let the Holy Spirit help you." Lexi tilted her head to one side. "Claire, when I was in that hospital waiting room, not knowing what was going to happen to my mom, God sent his Holy Spirit to give me more peace than I ever could have imagined. After experiencing him like that, there's no way I can*not* believe God is real and he loves me. That's what I want for you too."

Lexi took Claire's hand, squeezed, then let go. "We all make wrong choices and need Jesus to forgive us and help us be more like him. And the Holy Spirit is like a built-in best friend who never leaves, unlike some people." She looked at Claire knowingly. "So answer me as honestly as you can. Do you believe God is real and he loves you so much he let Jesus die to save you?"

Lexi saw tears filling the corners of Claire's closed eyes.

Claire took a deep breath and opened her eyes. Her gaze immediately found Lexi's as a smile played at her lips. "I do. I really do believe. And if God is as great as you make him sound, I definitely want to know him better."

Lexi squealed with delight as she threw her arms around Claire, nearly knocking them both to the floor. She steadied herself and sat back on her knees, turning serious again. "Can I pray for you right now?" She knew her words sounded confident, but inside she was shaking. She'd never asked anyone if she could pray for them right then and there. Thankfully, Claire nodded.

Lexi grabbed Claire's tense hand and this time, held on tight. They closed their eyes. "Dear God, thank you that Claire believes in you and wants to know you better. Thank you that she accepts Jesus as her savior, and please send your Holy Spirit to live inside her. Help Claire believe your promises, trust you, and know how much you love her. Let her believe that her that her dad moving out isn't her fault. Give her your strength and peace, and be Lord of her life. Thanks, God. Amen." Lexi finished and released Claire's hand, which now felt relaxed.

Claire paused. She inhaled deeply, her eyes closed. Lexi wished she would say something.

Finally, Claire opened her eyes and looked up at Lexi. She smiled, appearing more relaxed than she had in weeks. "So I'm officially a Christian now, aren't I? Thanks, Lexi. I do feel more peaceful about everything. God really is good." She glanced sideways. "But was there supposed to be some huge change after you prayed? Because I don't feel all *that* different."

Lexi smiled. "No, I don't think there is necessarily supposed to be a huge difference right away. Maybe it's different for everybody. I think the most important thing is that you trust in God and want the Holy Spirit to guide you now. And Claire—that's awesome! I'm so excited for you, and I'm so glad you came today! Thanks for letting me pray with you."

With huge smiles plastered on both their faces, they stood. Lexi gave Claire one more quick hug. "You ready to go downstairs and have some lunch?"

"Yes!" Claire exclaimed. The girls ran down the stairs and joined the rest of the family in the living room. Lexi's dad said grace, thanking God especially for his wife being home and Claire going to church with them.

As Lexi ate her chicken-fried steak, she looked around at so many people she loved sitting in the same room, and she felt full. Not full from the room temperature steak, fries, and okra (not yet anyway), but full of overwhelming love and thankfulness.

This month seemed like a whirlwind as she reflected back to her first class with Miss Kate. All the Holy Spirit homework, all of life's problems, and all of the spiritual growth that happened in her family seemed like it should have occurred over a lifetime, not just a month.

The ups and downs of raising her history grade so she could go to Six Flags with her class were over, and she could finally relax and look forward to her trip. She would definitely need to find a time to go shopping with her friends before the trip—she had outgrown last year's swimsuit and needed new sunglasses. (Millie had accidentally stepped on her old ones.)

Lexi was learning how to listen to the Holy Spirit more and more, her mom was getting better each day, and her entire family was learning to let the Holy Spirit be active in their lives. She knew the next six weeks or so would be difficult, as her mom continued to heal. She also knew she'd be doing a lot more chores around the house. But she was thankful, nonetheless.

Lexi prayed a quick, silent prayer of thanks to God for using Miss Kate to teach her entire family the truth about the Holy Spirit.

Grinning to herself, Lexi remembered the first day of class with Miss Kate. She had told the class they'd be going on a spiritual adventure together, but Lexi hadn't believed anything spiritual could be adventurous. Now, just a month later, each day had definitely become an adventure, and Lexi couldn't imagine life any other way.

"Lexi?" Her mom's voice snapped Lexi out of her thoughts and back to the conversation in the room. "Are you okay? You look like you're lost in outer space!"

Lexi laughed. "Sorry, Mom. I'm good, really. Do you need anything?"

"Other than a spleen?" she joked. Lexi smiled and rolled her eyes at her mother's attempt at humor.

"Nope, I don't need a thing," her mom went on. "I have everything I need right in this living room." She looked around from person to person, then winked at Lexi.

Lexi beamed with happiness, understanding exactly how her mom felt. And although Lexi was thrilled to look forward to the upcoming class trip, she knew now more than ever—there was nothing more she would ever need than to be surrounded by family and friends, with the Holy Spirit on her side.

APPENDIX

Your Six Flags Guide to Life with the Holy Spirit

1. First, decide to take the trip.

Sign up for this lifelong faith adventure by accepting Jesus as your Savior, like this:

- Admit you are a sinner—we all do wrong things that separate us from God's perfect goodness. (Romans 3:23)
- Believe God loves you so much he made a way for you to be with him for eternity, by sending his son Jesus to die as a sacrifice. (Romans 3:24-25)
- Be baptized and declare that Jesus is Lord of your life. (Acts 2:38, Philippians 2:10-11)

2. Invite your best friend!

Trips are always more fun with a friend! God, Jesus, and the Holy Spirit make up the *Trinity*—three beings in one. When you accept Jesus as your Savior, the Holy Spirit automatically moves in to live inside you. The Holy Spirit is always with you—like a built-in best friend! (Matthew 28:19, Ephesians 1:13, John 14:16)

3. Get going!

If you've accepted Jesus as your Savior, the Holy Spirit already lives in you—but *you* choose how active you allow him to be. Activate the Holy Spirit like this:

- Pray. Tell God you want to experience his Holy Spirit through prayer. Whether or not you speak in tongues or prophesy like some people, the Spirit will help you pray. (Acts 19:6, Romans 8:26-27)
- Listen. Ask him to speak to you, then listen and obey. (John 14:15)

- Believe. Have faith to believe he's always working for your own good and the good of others. (Romans 8:28)

4. Pick up a map when you arrive!

The Holy Spirit guides your way like a map by speaking directly to you, speaking through others, and helping you understand and apply what you read in the Bible. Let the Holy Spirit be your guide, and you'll never worry about losing your way. (Romans 8:14)

5. Visit the concession stand!

Just like you'll eventually need a refill on your fries or lemonade, you need to be refilled with the Holy Spirit from time to time. Yes, he lives inside you once you invite him in, but praying to be filled afresh will activate him in new ways and keep life exciting! (Acts 2:4 and 4:31)

6. Prepare for roller coasters!

Your faith journey will have ups and downs, just like a roller coaster. But whether you're up or down, the Holy Spirit is *always* your friend and helper. (Psalm 143:10)

NOTE TO THE READER:

If you're like many people (kids and adults), you may never have learned much about the Holy Spirit. Some of what you just read in *Power Up* might seem strange or confusing but let me assure you—experiencing the Holy Spirit is a completely natural part of being a Christian!

Picture a triangle with three equal sides. Can you imagine how those three sides are equally necessary parts of the triangle? If even one side was missing, it wouldn't be a triangle, right? In a similar way, while God is one complete *being*, he is made up of three *persons*, all at the same time.

1. He is God, our loving Father and Creator.
2. He is Jesus, who came to earth to save us from our sins.
3. He is the Holy Spirit, the Spirit who has resided with God and Jesus since the beginning of time, and who lives inside every Christian.

And guess what? Even though there are three persons of God (called the *Trinity*), they're all still God! Don't worry if it's confusing—this is tricky stuff to understand. The point is, not only can we develop a close, personal relationship with God and Jesus, but with the Holy Spirit too!

Another thing you may have noticed in *Power Up*, is that God and Jesus aren't mentioned as often as the Holy Spirit. That's simply because many people have heard about God and Jesus, but fewer have heard about the Holy Spirit—and he is very important, because through him, God himself lives inside us (his followers), to guide and empower us! In *Power Up*, the Holy Spirit had the spotlight but be assured—God and Jesus are just as important.

You can't see the Holy Spirit, but if you love God and follow Jesus, he already lives inside you! All you need to do is ask him to guide you and speak to you. (Sort of like the way we can't see the wind, but we know it's real because we feel it moving.)

If you haven't made the decision to become a Christian yet, I pray you'll stop and do so right now. If you want, you can pray this prayer:

> *Dear God, I believe in you. I know you created me and love me, but I also know I make bad choices and sin sometimes. Thank you for sending Jesus to take the punishment for my sins. Please forgive the wrong things I do and help me make better choices that honor you. I want Jesus to be Lord of my life. Send your Holy Spirit to guide and help me every day. I love you, God. Amen.*

If you just prayed that prayer for the first time, CONGRATULATIONS! Heaven is celebrating *you* right now! Whether you're a Christian or not, you might have a lot of questions after reading this book. Asking questions is always good, so I encourage you to find a pastor or a trusted adult who loves Jesus and ask away!

No matter where you are on your journey with God, after you accept Jesus, my prayer is for you to engage with the Holy Spirit and POWER UP!

ABOUT THE AUTHOR

Jessie Mattis grew up between cornfields in Potomac, Illinois with an ever changing stack of library books beside her bed. Children, reading, writing, and God have been major parts of life as long as she can remember, so when the inspiration for Power Up struck, it seemed only natural to run with the idea. Jessie graduated from Greenville College with a BA in social work and worked several years in the field of foster care and adoption before becoming a full-time mom. She and her family were part of a church planting team several years ago, which planted Rolling Hills Vineyard Church in Valparaiso, Indiana. She gained many invaluable lessons and insights through this experience.

Jessie lives with her husband and fellow author, Chip Mattis, and their three amazing kids in Bloomington, Indiana, and immensely enjoys being a wife and mom. While she is often busy homeschooling the kids, you can also find her spending time with friends and family, serving at church, reading, writing, or sneaking chocolate from the cupboard to go with her black coffee (when the kids aren't looking, of course).

Jessie's debut novel, Power Up, was an award winner in the 2018 Blue Ridge Mountains Christian Writers Conference annual contest.

Connect with Jessie through social media or on her website at www.jessiemattis.com – she would love to hear from you!

CPSIA information can be obtained
at www.ICGtesting.com
Printed in the USA
LVHW080801180722
723744LV00022B/553

9 781950 051632